OF KIDS & PARENTS

EMIL HAKL

OF KIDS & PARENTS

Translated from the Czech by Marek Tomin

TWISTED SPOON PRESS • PRAGUE • 2008

ISBN 978-80-86264-30-1

This translation was made possible by a grant from
the Ministry of Culture of the Czech Republic

H

I hear slippers in an absurd hallway leading to
my heart.

FERNANDO PESSOA

Behold his eyes the tears for no one came,
two years reclused in a desert he stayed,
and thrice a day when the chapel's bells tolled,
they all would say: Oh, the sad youth does ring!

FROM AN OLD WOODCUT

"See who?" asked the old man in the gatehouse, cupping his ear. He didn't look at me because he was busy carefully cutting something and arranging the slices on a greasy piece of paper.

"Mr. Beneš," I repeated.

"And who's that?"

"One of your employees."

"Why don't you give him a call then," he said, pushing a phone towards me, still not looking up.

"Greetings Dad," I said into the foul-smelling receiver.

"Yeah, hi, listen, could you wait for me? I've got a tour to do in a minute but I'll be right over in less than an hour. Go check out the snakes or something for a while."

"Okay," I said.

The old man stuck a slice of greenish brawn in his mouth and began chewing vigorously.

I reached the Penguin House and walked in. The black and white birds were marching one behind the other in a line along the concrete edge of the pool. One of them suddenly had the idea to launch itself sideways into the water. The others immediately toppled over behind the first one, zooming around underwater for a moment like broken homing torpedoes. Then one of them decided to dart out of the water and the others followed, forming a neat line. Then the whole procedure began all over again. One penguin always got the idea to jump in a fraction of a second earlier than the rest and before it had even hit the water's surface they were all plopping in. They repeated this over and over for the entire hour I stood there. I could easily have stayed for another hour but it was time to go back.

Father stood motionless in front of the gatehouse and although it was still summer he was wearing a white raincoat and a ratty peaked cap which he called the "Prince Heinrich." He'd been on a pension for a few years and was earning extra cash as a tour guide at the zoo, escorting school kids, groups of tourists from Ústí nad Labem, and Dutch pensioners on theme tours, patiently expounding on sea lions and wildebeest and waiting while they had a good romp at the Monkey House. I was startled at how much more his hair had greyed during the few weeks since I'd last seen him.

"Hi," I said.

"Hi there," he answered, his eyes fixed on a point somewhere beyond the treetops.

"So what's new?" I asked.

"Nothing's been new in this world for more than two billion years, it's all just variations on the same theme of carbon, hydrogen, helium, and nitrogen," Father answered.

We set out on a walk. Or to be more precise, we walked around Troja Chateau, crossed over the footbridge, from which I spat into the dense, slowly rolling waters of the Vltava River, then across Imperial Island, and over another footbridge, from which Father let fall a long white trail of saliva into the dense, slowly rolling waters of the canal. Then we entered Stromovka Park.

"For goodness' sake, why do you of all people always ask what's new?" Father said in time to his strides. "That's such a difficult question, in fact it's the most difficult of all! Now, if you had asked me how I am, that I would know . . ."

"Well, how are you, then?"

"Not well . . . But come to think of it I do have some news, an orangutan went missing recently, we've got these students helping us out at the moment and one of the girls probably forgot to close the door to the cage properly during feeding time and, well, the orangutan disappeared. So we started looking for him, we combed the whole zoo, every nook and cranny, every bush, but couldn't find him anywhere, the director even called the police but they told him to get lost, so we kept looking. It wasn't till the third day when everyone was getting desperate that Tonda Siňor, the guy who prepares the food for the monkeys, realised a bottle of wine he'd left open on the table when he'd gone to take a leak a couple of days before was empty, but he hadn't drunk it. So just to make sure, they rifled through the cellar a second time and that's when they found him. The orangutan, God bless his soul, had crawled under a pile of wood wool and was sleeping contentedly, so they woke him up, took a blood sample and discovered he'd drunk the wine . . . Damn, I hope it's not going to rain . . ."

We were walking through Stromovka Park. Skinny guys in their fifties with cropped hair and dubious suntans were cruising around on roller-blades between the patches of grass. Dogs were chasing each other in the grass. Even though it was only four in the afternoon, the windows of the palace on the park's hill were illuminated by the light of chandeliers.

"If we take that path over there, walk through the little tunnel and up the hill, we'll end up right in front of The Royal Park," I said.

"And what are we going to do there?"

"It's a pub."

"Oh okay, let's go then, I don't know the place so at least I'll get to know it," Father said. "Another time we misplaced a chimpanzee and no matter how hard we tried we just couldn't find it. And the police? They said it was none of their business, but when they got a call from a granny who lives in Troja, telling them there was a blind-drunk guy dancing and jumping on the roof opposite her house and asking them to do something about it before he got himself killed, they were there in a flash and you know what? It wasn't a drunk, it was our chimp, the old woman's eyesight wasn't so good anymore. It took quite an effort to catch him and get him back into his cage, poor fellow! The police know how to push people around, that's for sure, but when it's time to help a poor animal . . . People steal *parrots*, for goodness' sake! And what do the police do? Though on the other hand they did give us back that ant . . ."

"What ant?"

"Oh, you know the story."

"No I don't, tell me."

"I told you that story, didn't I? About that great big iron ant that sits on the lawn on the way to the Bear House. It disappeared without a trace. They brought it back a year later, out of the blue, they'd found it in some drug den, hadn't been looking for it or anything, just chanced upon it during a raid on these youngsters. Seems they had it hidden somewhere in a shed where they did drugs and apparently they *worshipped* it in some way, or something like that . . . Anyway, they'd painted it all over with different colours so we had to get thinner and scrub it down with a steel brush."

Father stopped and stared at some reeds growing out of the bank of a muddy pond.

"Well, look at that . . . ," he remarked.

A reed was swaying gently. A rigid, greenish-brown cone was poking out from its side. Pond skaters were skimming over the still surface of the water. In the distance, a train tooted.

"You know what that is?" Father asked.

"A reed of some kind," I said.

"Reed indeed, that's a *sweet flag!*"

"Maybe."

"Not 'maybe,' it is, sweet flag, Latin name *Acorus*, otherwise known as flagroot, originally from south China, now common in our country, but for one reason only — the Tatars brought it here."

"Oh, right."

"They used it to test water to see if it was okay to drink."

"Right, and how did they do that?"

"It happened like this: the sentries, the scouts came ahead of everyone else and when they found water they threw the root of the sweet flag in it, waited a few days, people weren't in such a hurry back then, and if the sweet flag set down roots they took it as proof the water was safe to drink. After that the hordes could arrive and continue to burn and pillage at their leisure. That's also why the sweet flag used to be known as *Tatar Grass*. Every Tatar worthy of the name back in the days of Genghis Khan carried koumiss, dried meat, and sweet flag!"

"A while back a friend and I were making absinthe and in addition to the wormwood, sweet woodruff and other herbs we also used dried sweet flag, but you have to be really careful because it's so damned bitter it overpowers everything else," I recollected.

"Well that's typical, all your stories always end up on one or two subjects," Father sighed. "And what did it taste like?"

"To tell the truth, it was disgusting."

"There you go," Father said.

We ascended slowly up the leaf-strewn paths towards The Royal Park. We opened the door and entered. A few afternoon customers were sitting in the pub. As soon as we sat down the waiter hurried over.

"Two beers and a bite to eat," Father said, taking a wad of crumpled newspaper cuttings out of his satchel and handing them to me. "This is for you . . ."

It was another portion of newspaper articles: WHAT'S HAP-PENING BEYOND OUR SOLAR SYSTEM; YES! I REALLY WAS A SPY; SCIENTISTS DISCOVER A NEW SPECIES OF SQUID; WHY THE CREW OF THE KURSK COULDN'T ESCAPE ON ITS OWN; WOMEN ARE APPARENTLY GENETICALLY PREDISPOSED TO BEING REPROACHFUL and THE OLD SPARKLE OF KLÁNOVICE IS RETURNING. I became absorbed in the piece about Klánovice.

"What they omitted to mention, however, is that Klánovice is also the place where the famous composer R.A. Dvorský had his villa," Father noted from over the edge of the grimy menu, "which is where he bought a song called 'The Gypsy Girl,' from Vacek, whom he'd invited to dinner, for three hundred crowns, which was quite a sum before the war of course, and once 'The Gypsy Girl' had become a big hit, apparently Vacek tore his hair out, which is about all he could do by then, you know ... At least that's what my father used to claim, though who knows if it's actually true, he liked to tell stories about how people became millionaires, about people struck by good fortune ... But the only real millionaire he used to see a lot of in Klánovice after the war was a guy by the name of Papež, I believe he had a shoe company on Na Příkopech Street, and also a man called Pučelík, who made liqueur, you know, *Pučelík's Little Happiness Liqueur,* it was a popular drink at the time ..."

"I remember Pučelík, a crooked old codger who used to wear a hat and a long coat! He had a bamboo walking stick stained black from all the handling and every third step he'd jab forward with it, piercing the air ..."

"Mildorf and Fadrhonc and Rylek, they were all old men by the time you were born, but they were really nouveau riche types who were unlucky because they hadn't left the country in time. Papež was the only real millionaire, and then this fellow Pučelík."

"I remember Rylek as well! He was a fat, merry fellow with a huge head!"

"Of course you remember him, he used to come over every other day to argue with my father about what would have happened if the Communists hadn't taken over ..."

"His cheeks were like melons and he wore a beautifully embroidered *tubeteika,* a Tatar cap, on that head of his and when he laughed he roared so hard he'd almost choke!"

"That's right, though he didn't wear a tubeteika, but one of those ordinary woolly hats with a snake-like zigzag pattern, what everyone calls a *zmijovka* . . . He was also an old Sokol member and likely an old alcoholic as well, but for some unknown reason he liked you. He used to call you *Charl*."

"Not Charl, Charles," I said.

"Okay . . . Could you please read this for me? I forgot my glasses."

"Well, they've got goulash," I said, taking the sticky plastic coated menu in my hands, "probably don't want that, right, so then there's . . ."

"What was the first thing?"

"Goulash."

"Kolache?"

"Goulash!!!"

"Well keep your hair on, goulash, no, I won't have that. What else?"

"Then there's schnitzel with potatoes."

"Might as well shoot me in the head!"

"Then there's Szeged stew and djulbastia . . ."

"Djulbastia with a long 'a' for goodness' sake, it hails from the Balkans, no one knows how to cook that here, they probably mean some sort of chevapchichi . . . But no one here knows how to cook that either . . ."

"Then there's Devil's Pocket."

"What?"

"Devil's Pocket," I said, my voice shaking.

"Sorry, my hearing's playing up, what they serve these days, really . . . What's a Devil's Pocket?"

"Well, I don't know, it's a Devil's Pocket, that's all!"

"You know, you're more irritable than my father, he also hated for anybody to ask him anything . . ."

On such occasions, the frequency of Father's voice, although not unreasonably loud, exactly fills the gap between the pitch of a normal conversation and an argument. Worse still, it takes on a kind of public, demonstrative quality. Most of the pub couldn't help but notice. Damn, at least don't shout! I've wanted to say to him for years, but have always kept my mouth shut.

"Then there's fish fillet," I said.

"Ah, *fish fillet!*" Father bellowed at the whole room, staring out at the clouds with a painful expression on his face, "but it should say what *kind of fish* . . ."

"What kind of fish!" I said under my breath, "the kind that swims in water!"

"Ah, but it's not that simple . . ." Father smiled, "could be Alaskan cod or sea bass, could be hake, *Merluccius merluccius*, or seawolf, *Anarhicas lupus* . . . Oh well, never mind, it'll probably be cod or haddock . . ."

"Most likely."

"Well, don't get upset, I'll have the fish fillet."

"I'm not upset," I said in the direction of the window, blood pounding in my temples, the whole world wobbling before my eyes. The waiter brought the fish fillet.

Father took a tiny nibble. "Don't get angry, I just need to know what I'm eating and then I'll basically eat anything . . . yeah, it's cod alright . . . I remove the tiny skeletons from sardines and sprats, though, which some might find a bit ridiculous, and I don't eat sweetbread, but otherwise I'll eat anything."

"I'm not angry, I just eat what they bring me, that's all."

"But so do I, when I was in Holland they gave us this strange cucumber stuffed with fish and cream sauce to go with it, everyone was surreptitiously handing it back, I was the only one to actually eat it and I really enjoyed it too! And because it wasn't a huge portion I had some dry rice to fill me up. And there was a Japanese fellow there from Tokyo and he was laughing at me from a distance — what does that guy want, I thought to myself — and he kept on laughing and in the end he came over and said: 'Mister, you eating dry rice? You are just like us, mister, we also eat dry rice, not because we have to but because we like it!' "

Then Father became absorbed in his food. In the meanwhile, I was checking out why the crew of the Kursk submarine was unable to escape on its own. As usual, I was most intrigued by the diagram of the whole situation with all sorts of boats floating on the surface and sending variously equipped divers below on unreasonably thick cables, as well as robots and mini-subs, and in the depths there was the gloomy cigar-shaped object with the crushed bow.

"You know, I was thinking the other day . . ." Father said, putting down his cutlery, "and I realised that all my life the people I've known, the women, Ivana, Růžena, everybody, have always whined to me about things, and I can't recall ever having complained to anybody . . ."

"I'm not complaining," I said the first stupid thing my brain transmitted to me.

"*Not now*, but I remember when you were breaking up with, what's her name, you know, that Marta, I had to force several shots of gin down your throat before the blood returned to your face, you were so miserable."

"For God's sake, that was eighteen years ago or something," I objected.

"Well, that may be, but people complain to me day after day!"

"Do some moaning yourself, then," I suggested.

"Easy for you to say, I don't even know how it's done."

"All you have to do is whine and moan, though in the end you have to make people think that it's all somehow beneath you."

"The last time I tried that was when I started seeing your mother. Young people can complain, that's acceptable, but when an old man starts to whine he should get a sound beating . . ."

Beyond the half-open window stiletto heels were clicking on the dusty pavement. We both turned towards the sound. A girl in a red sweater was walking down the street blowing a bubble with gum. A girl called Iveta or Ilona, no doubt. The bubble grew huge, finally bursting and sticking to her left cheek.

"I'd give three thousand crowns from my pension to some young lass just to be able to give *her tits a good squeeze* one more time in my life!" Father said all of a sudden. It came out disproportionately loud, and what's more it was during a momentary lull in the pub chatter. Several customers raised their heads.

"More beer, gentlemen?" the waiter rushed over.

"Give us two vodkas," Father said without realising he'd just been complaining.

We clinked glasses.

"You know, people in this country are getting spoilt for food," Father continued, "back in Yugoslavia the standard fare was *zhganci*, they're like long yellow dumplings made from corn flour and with them you had either sauce or cheese, cream cheese or bacon fat, or you could also have them with something sweet, but the basic element was zhganci . . . When we lived in Zagreb, there was a textiles factory down below our house with this long

19

lawn in front of it, and around noon the workers would always sit on the lawn and have lunch, I used to watch them from the window because there were some attractive women among them, I was eight or nine at the time. These workmen always ate the same thing, corn bread with onions and some of them, *only a few mind you*, had bacon fat to go with it, and that's what they ate, all the time, every day, all week and the whole month! The slaves who built the pyramids in Egypt, they had it even worse, all they had to eat were millet pancakes, onions, and beer."

"Right, and further east people are even less demanding," I said. "In India there's a particular sadhu sect that's still active today despite thousands of years of persecution, and these sadhus secretly hang around near cemeteries on the banks of the Ganges . . ."

"Uh, I wonder what kind of filth I'm going to learn about now . . ."

"Nothing original, in short they live off the human flesh thrown into the water after a burial ceremony. They grab the bodies downstream and eat the flesh. It's already been roasted but mostly it's also gone rancid and rotten and they love that because they do it for religious reasons, and when you've got religious reasons then no filth is filthy enough."

"Might as well join them, I'm on a strict fat-free diet on account of my gall bladder, I can only eat food that's been boiled or cooked without fat . . . What about that magazine *Aviation*, still buying it?"

"Yeah," I said, "but more out of habit these days, although sometimes they have interesting articles. Last year, for example, there was a long article about the Ki-44 Shoki . . . or was that the year before last?"

"You always did like ugly airplanes."

"Come on, the Ki-44 is not ugly!"

"Maybe, but you used to like ugly airplanes . . . and the one you liked most was the Sparviero!"

"Well, I liked the way it's crooked like an old beggar, that it's got three propellers and there's something naïve about it. But that was when I was really young!"

"What are you talking about, the last time we walked through the woods to Ouvaly you were fond of the Sparviero, and that was about ten years ago, you weren't young then . . ."

"Never mind, it doesn't matter, so I like the Sparviero," I said, waving my hand astonished at the fact that this particular conversation has always infuriated me.

"But you know the Sparviero wasn't a bad plane," Father said, setting out on a well-trodden path, "it was a little short on motor power like all Italian models but as a torpedo bomber it was more than useful, given that it was in fact a prewar mixed construction . . . Even the Pipistrello was a pretty good plane for its time. You know what *pipistrello* means in Italian?"

"Yes I do."

"Sure you do, *bat*, what are you frowning about?"

"Because you need to pontificate all the time."

"*Me?* Pontificate?"

"All the time!"

"And how, might I ask, do I do that?"

"Everything you say starts or ends with a lecture!"

"Well, there you go. I guess it's just my way of . . ."

"But what sort of a conversation does that make!"

"Conversations are an illusion, everyone on earth wants to talk about his own thing and, if at all possible, all the time!"

"I'm not so sure about that."

"That's because you haven't grown up yet."

"You've been telling me that for thirty years."

"Well, it's been true for thirty years."

"Yeah, two more," I told the waiter.

At that moment, a guy called Kulich walked into the pub in a periwinkle-green leather jacket, said hello to everyone in a sweeping gesture, even though no one even looked up at him, leant on the bar and began scanning the customers. When he got to me, he said Heeeeey and showed signs of moving away from the bar till he noticed Father. He stayed standing where he was. I'd known Kulich since the days when I used to spend a lot of time on Letná.

"You liked the Sparviero alright," Father nodded, "you were always keen on the ugliest airplanes, stumpy and fat, the Henschel 123, Fiat CR.42, wildcat, hellcat, bearcat, and then that sort of two-tailed slipper-shaped plane, the F7U Cutlass, you loved that one . . . I liked planes like the Mosquito, for example, that was my ideal!"

"The Mosquito looks like a dildo, how could you like it!" I said.

"Well, it's got a pronounced *aerodynamic* shape, an economical and purposeful design!"

"I find those generally-liked designs insulting. In that sense I really do prefer the Sparviero," a cantankerous demon started waking up inside me, taking over my mind, as always happened sooner or later when having a discussion with Father.

"Well, what did I say!" Father retorted.

"I like airplanes that are exceptional in some way, that aren't boring at first sight, it's the same with women."

"There you go, though I don't quite get your comparison."

"Well, a woman is interesting if, first of all, she's resourceful and, secondly, marked by life a little, right?" I said, trying to lower my voice because I was watching Kulich, who in the meanwhile had moved to a table by the window. Whenever my eyes moved in his direction he started nodding as if to reassure me. Nodding and whistling through his teeth like a teenager.

"I can't agree with you there," Father said.

I know that, the little demon inside me jabbered: You always liked the worst kind . . . ! I remember those cold bimbos! Those stupid polished fashion models . . . ! The student types . . . always laughing . . . ! Those big-lipped Mahulenas . . . ! Ones with fake accents! And anyway, whatever happened to our house in Klánovice . . . !? You blew it! You drank it away . . . ! We didn't have to be left on the breadline! I know that much!

"Doesn't matter," I said under my breath, "I just wouldn't even park my bike next to one of those smooth pinup girls from *Penthouse*, one of those *dumb bimbos!* And as for airplanes, it's the same thing. I just like it when you can see some effort's gone into the design, some sense of counterpoise, compromise, development! Take the piston Corsairs, for instance, especially the F4U-5 or the AU-1, those were beautiful planes, the peak of what was possible during the propeller era, several hundred k an hour, four twenty-millimetre cannons and yet no banal aerodynamics. Gorgeous!"

"The Corsair's got wings like a seagull that's been run over by a car," grumbled Father, upholding the principle that in a debate the two sides always have to hold opposite opinions, "and I'd be very surprised about that seven hundred, six hundred and fifty maybe, max!"

"The 5 was a little slower," I finally allowed myself to get fully absorbed in an essentially male discussion. Adrenalin was on its way and there was no denying my pulse was up. "But the AU-1 did seven hundred at three thousand metres!"

"I'm not sure about that . . . In any case the model M Thunderbolt was at least a 100 k faster with the same motor, but with water injection directly into the cylinders and a different turbo-compressor!"

"No way a 100, 50 maybe, but look at the cost! For starters, the short lifespan of that cranked-up motor, and secondly the Thunderbolt looked like a tree stump with wings!"

"On the ground, maybe. But in the air it was fabulous . . . At the end of the war I was walking down a street in Zagreb and suddenly I heard a terrible roar. I looked around, couldn't see anything, and then a Thunderbolt flew low over the roofs, all guns blazing, and because it was flying so low cartridges were falling all around me onto the pavement, ringing like bells, one fell right in front of me, so I picked it up and burnt myself, it was that hot," Father started reminiscing. "But what I wanted to say was that it then got some height and circled around the train station as though it was light as a feather, like some little silver bird, just fluttering in the air, even though it weighed seven tons . . . But the first airplane I ever saw during the war was a German Dornier Do 17, known as the flying pencil, it was flying high above Zagreb and the Yugoslavs were firing at it with cannons, the sun was shining, the sky was blue, and I was watching from the balcony, there were these tiny grey puffs of cloud behind it made by the shells exploding and I thought to myself *the war isn't all that bad!* But it was different later, when the Allies started flying sorties over us, one wave after another," Father said, taking a swig of beer.

In the meantime, I was watching the way Kulich was scrutinising us. The way he was trying to guess the subject of our conversation in that routine manner of a life-long pub rocker. The way he was chewing on his toothpick. The way he was squinting at us. The way he turned towards us with his whole body, fitting tightly into his leather jacket embellished with an enormous number of zips and pockets. Maybe it hadn't been such a good idea to have come to The Royal Park.

"And another time the siren went off," Father continued, "my mother had just finished roasting a chicken and she was taking it to the table, we no longer even bothered going to the shelter because the Americans always just flew by. But suddenly right above us bombers appeared in formation, really beautifully aerodynamic B-26 Marauders, flying real low, the air was pulsating like this, my father didn't hesitate and just jumped off the terrace into the bushes and then we heard that very specific sound, just like slag dropping off a truck, and that was the bombs falling. And when it was over, the textile works down the road were burning, smoke everywhere, our windows had all shattered and your grandma was shaking her fist at them and swearing because the chicken had fallen on the carpet."

"Fact is, I remember that my whole childhood we ate chicken all the time. We had porridge for breakfast and once in a while we had that sort of chocolate layer-cake made from Carslbad wafers, which was really tasty."

"You're right about that, but you had to let it sit for a couple of days before eating it."

"That's right! So it'd be nice and spongy!" I said and glimpsed Kulich nodding in agreement. Nodding and now continuously squinting. Although he surely couldn't understand a thing we were saying since he was sitting five metres away.

"Well, towards the end my mother didn't feel like cooking too often, but back in Yugoslavia she used to cook a lot of different meals," Father said.

"But you said you mostly ate those corn dumplings," I objected and couldn't help noticing that Kulich was nodding again. It was starting to make me a little nervous.

"Our family not as much, really," Father admitted, "because Father was a gourmet, his favourite meal was marinated tuna with almonds and olives, or boiled lobster just with onions and drizzled with virgin olive oil, I lost my appetite for it back then because we had it all the time and nowadays I feel like crying just thinking about it . . . He also liked stuffed poultry with polenta, but you should have seen those hens, they were something else! Mother used to make lard from them. People here laugh when they hear that, but poultry lard spread on a piece of bread was so good, you just couldn't stop eating it, it was just as smooth as duck lard but had a special kind of taste, maybe she added some other ingredient, I don't know," Father said, and his Adam's apple bobbed up and down conspicuously.

"I remember the first thing in my life that surprised me was seeing Granddad picking carp eyes out of fish soup and sucking on them," I said.

Over by the window, Kulich raised his glass to let me know that although he didn't know what we were talking about, if the bearded old codger and I were having a little dispute or something, then as a matter of principle he would likely take my side.

"Oh yes, he liked that," Father nodded. "But there was another thing I wanted to tell you, about how brave my mother was at the time . . . There was a kind of meadow in front of our apartment and every night drunks from the pub, which was right next door to us, would fight on this meadow — makes you wonder though, what kind of bright idea it was to live right next door to a pub . . . There was always a dreadful racket, but not like here in Bohemia, after every fight down there at least three or four people were left bleeding on the grass all night, their throats rattling, cursing and calling to each other, though oddly enough come morning there was no one there, though Father had to hose the blood off the grass every time. Often it was like some gruesome fairy tale, like when this guy ran out of the pub cursing and bolted off somewhere and in a moment he was back with a double-edged dagger, known as a kindjal, in his hand. And a small guy with a moustache, probably an Ustashi agent because he was holding a stubby Beretta pistol, came out towards him and said in a shrill voice: *'Move away!'*, but then another guy clonked the little guy over the head with a truncheon from behind and he fell down flat on his face, they took his gun, and laughing, firing over their heads, they disappeared into the night . . . But the reason I'm telling you this is that one time they were beating the hell out of each other again and your grandmother suddenly became furious, went outside and shouted: 'Stop that racket for once, our child is sleeping, so quit that fighting or I'm coming out and you'll be sorry!' "

"In Czech?"

"In Croatian, of course."

"And what child did she mean?"

"Well, she meant me . . . I was already ten years old by then, but Mother always had her ideals, she meant that *it could easily happen* that a small child might be sleeping there and then what!

When my father saw how my mother was getting ready to go out between those murderers he got scared and went to find his gun, he had an unlicensed 9 calibre Mauser, but he was so agitated he couldn't find it and when he did he couldn't find the cartridges, and before he could load it the men had run off because the whole episode was so irrational they all got scared . . . The police were afraid to deal with that place, but your grandmother gave them such a fright they ran for it."

"And why did you guys come back to Bohemia after the war?"

"The thing was that Father joined Tito's army in the last year of the war, him — a factory owner — and no one could talk him out of it! He joined the Partisans to serve in the *thirteenth proletarian army*, as he never failed to point out . . . But when the war was over the executions and prison sentences began anew because the great comrade Tito began settling accounts with his enemies, first it was the former gendarmes, the monarchists, you know, and then Communists started getting rid of Communists, as always happens everywhere, you know, it's always the same story, the only difference between events of this kind is the way they're later interpreted. And the history of the Balkans is sombre and full of pathos like a German opera, it's no laughing matter, there are always rivers of blood, severed heads roll about in the streets, and right next to them people dance and brass bands play."

"Who the hell knows if that's not better in the end than the slow, dreary variety show they put on here."

"The only reason you can even say that is because you don't know what it's like when someone down the road is actually cutting someone else's throat, or when they hang an entire family, children included, right in front of your eyes . . . What was it you were asking me, oh yes, why our family came back. Well, for one thing, immediately after the war they started nationalising and even though my father had a few perks on account of his activities in the resistance and they let him sell the factory, in other words he didn't lose absolutely everything, even so he'd had just about enough of it. His idea was to come back to Bohemia and set up a tie-making factory with his cousin Vilda, all he ever talked about was how he and Vilda were going to have a *little tie factory* and how they were going to live in peace and quiet. So they sent me to Prague in 1945, I didn't really want to go, I wanted to go to the naval academy, didn't I . . . So my parents came up in 1948 and within two years the Communists had thrown my father in prison and I'd gone to work in a factory."

"Hmm, that's the way it goes."

"Exactly, you'd think people would learn their lesson, but they never do, especially not here in Bohemia. That's why my father wanted to return, on account of this pipedream about a land of milk and honey that all the Czechs in Yugoslavia had envisaged in a fixated sort of way, they kept sighing about how great it was going to be when Doctor Beneš and his wife Hana returned to Prague Castle and they'd have sausage and Pilsner beer and go for a stroll in Stromovka Park . . . And about Honza Masaryk, you know, and how Churchill won't let Stalin take . . . and so on and so on."

"*Churchill* was one of the first words I registered as a child, *Churchill* and *Khrushchev.*"

"Well, they were always at it, my mother and father, always arguing about politics. But the first word you spoke was *father*, I remember that well, because your mother refused to talk to me all day as a result, somehow she got offended."

"I didn't even know that."

"How could you, you were a year old . . . What were we talking about? Oh yeah, my father! Well, basically, he was just tired, that's all, he started out in Yugoslavia back in the '20s and initially he lost everything two or three times and had to start again from scratch until he finally set himself up . . . He was tired alright."

"What made him want to go to Yugo in the first place?"

"He was the youngest of four children, three of whom were brothers and so he got some money from his father to start him off and went out into the world to make his fortune, that's how it was. Even being born on a farm didn't help, being the youngest he was given money and off he went, that was the custom back then. And why Croatia? To tell you the truth, I don't rightly know why he went there, but a lot of Czechs did in those days. I guess they saw it as a land of opportunity."

I stood up to go to the loo. As I did I brushed against my satchel, it keeled over on its side and a book slid out.

"Oh look, what are you reading?" said Father, bending down.

"I'm not actually reading it, I just carry it around with me."

I walked across the pub and turned onto the ramp leading to the loo. I'd barely positioned myself above the urinal when Kulich was by my side, staring at the tiles and chewing loudly. Close up I realised that he, too, was almost an old man, if it weren't for the earrings and chains and ponytail. That if he shed those ornaments of youth, an ordinary proper citizen with a big nose and beer gut would be standing next to me.

"Who's the bloke?" he inquired.

"That's my dad."

"You guys go out drinking together, do you?"

"Yeah."

"How often?"

"About once every three weeks."

"*With your dad*, really?"

"That's right, and?"

"Oh nothing, mate, all good . . . And you guys *have a good banter together*, do you?"

"That's right, an ordinary conversation. It's also got its downsides."

"Yeah, I guess it does . . . Talk about women, do you?"

"A little bit, yeah."

"Hey, could I come over and sit with you guys for a bit?"

"Well, we're leaving in a minute."

"Just for a bit, I'm waiting for Jirka, there's some bands from the north playing at Slamník tonight . . ."

"Sorry Kulich, but not tonight, thanks."

"Well, if you say so, then . . . He's really your dad, is he?"

"Yeah."

When I came back, shaking my wet hands in the air, Father was thumbing through the book, shaking his head and reading out loud: "*Whatever the precise nature of the question of the mystery of being may be, it is certainly very complicated, or it may in fact be very simple, if the nature of this simplicity is such that we are unable to perceive it . . .*" for crying out loud, that doesn't make any sense whatsoever, it's philosophy or something, never did like that sort of highfalutin literature . . ."

"Neither do I, but sometimes it's the only way not to be alone," I said quietly.

"Besides specialised literature, over the last few years I've been quite happy just reading Hašek, Shakespeare, and crime novels, but nowadays even Shakespeare pisses me off, though some parts still strike me as genius."

Whatever you do, don't start reciting . . . I said a silent prayer to myself: Not now . . . ! Not here . . . ! Especially not Shakespeare! There's no need . . . ! Be quiet . . . !

"Yet better thus, and known to be contemned, than still contemned and flattered. The lowest and most dejected thing of fortune, stands still in esperance, lives not in fear . . ." Father began to declaim in an unnaturally high, piercing mewl.

Be silent . . . Shut up . . . I felt like screaming: Shut it! For God's sake! Don't yell!

"Welcome, then, thou unsubstantial air that I embrace! The wretch that thou hast blown unto the worst owes nothing to thy blasts . . . !"

I was smiling sweetly and could feel the eyes of the whole pub staring at me. Fuck them, I roared in my head, who cares about them, you're sitting here with an old man and that's that. The old fart's drunk and he's railing on, they're all thinking, that's okay, but what about that other dickhead? Is he a faggot? Druggie? Loon? I saw Kulich ceremoniously giving me the thumbs up from halfway across the room, like he's rooting for me.

"How about we move on, walk a bit more?" I suggested.

"Sure, we can do that," Father said, lowering his voice. "Boy was I glad to get a chance to read Joyce's *Ulysses* back when I had my pancreas operated on, Iva brought it over to the hospital, because I'd asked her to bring some really thick book, I'd meant something like Melville or Victor Hugo, I'd even have enjoyed reading Kipling again after so many years, but Iva just took all the thick books off the shelf, looked at them and put the thickest in her bag and that turned out to be a copy of *Ulysses*, which some-one had forgotten at my place at some point . . . It wasn't you by any chance, was it?"

"No, I've got my copy at home. I've started reading it two or

three times over the years but have given up every time somewhere around page fifty."

"Oh well, I finished it, you know I was reading it so *attentively*,
like nothing before because I was thinking that it might just be
the last thing I get to read in this world! I was taking in every
word, not that I understood any of it, but at the time I didn't care
. . . This sort of literature — what's called belles lettres — is
mainly for people who otherwise don't get a lot out of life, it's for
miserable bastards, you know. Everybody else, those who are
healthy and have money, they only look at it as a bit of light,
tedious entertainment before falling asleep."

"That's true," I said.

"But lately, whenever I find even a *postcard* or just a *utilities bill*
in my box it gives me joy and I read it carefully, word by word,
because as I do I'm clearly aware of still being alive . . ."

We left the pub and, walking along the line of the hill, we reached the Governor's Palace.

"So where to now?" Father asked nonchalantly, his voice directed towards the battlement-like row of tiny housing blocks on the horizon. Behind the hill, spattered with the white cubes of buildings, an unbroken ridge of clouds was slowly advancing.

"I guess the best thing is to go back to Stromovka, if you don't mind."

"I don't mind anything, as long as it doesn't rain," Father said and, rolling up his sleeve, fished a packet of Marlboro out of his pocket, lit one on the third attempt and held it in front of him awkwardly, blowing the smoke towards the mass of lukewarm August air surging out of the valley.

We walked down and then across the grassy basin of the park. Eventually we reached the river again and set out along its bank towards Podbaba, striding along the straight and desolate Za Elektrárnou Street. To our left rustled the park and to our right the muddy waters of the canal splashed onto rocks. Ducks were paddling diligently against the current. The drakes were proudly swaying their pretty, somewhat stupid blue-green heads from side to side. Seagulls were pecking at bits of bread-roll and dead slime-coated rats bobbing in the water.

Suddenly our noses were struck by a thick, pungent stench.

"No way that's just some rotting mouse," Father remarked.

We could feel the almighty reek lining and clinging to our mucous membranes. We accelerated and tried to walk through it.

"I'll just take a look, see what it might be," I decided purely out of curiosity.

"Oh forget it and come on."

"You go ahead, I'll catch up," I said, taking a good deep breath and walking back a few steps. A cloud of flies hovered above the bushes. A black roll of tarpaper covered by discarded planks and branches lay in the bushes. A formless round object was rolled up inside it. In the half-light I could see something inside the cylinder. With a slight stretch of the imagination it could have been a sweater wrapped around something with caked black hair, but might just as well have been, and probably was, the fur of some animal. I turned around and caught up with Father, who was walking along resolutely.

"So?" he asked.

"A dog, I guess."

For a while we walked in silence.

"Near the end of the war, when they were showering Zagreb with bombs, every now and then they'd hit a residential block and because there wasn't enough time to clean up the mess, entire streets stank exactly like that, it was almost unbearable, and that smell has bothered me ever since," Father said.

"Oh."

"But people even get used to things like that after a while, if they last long enough, but the one thing I still have dreams about to this day is an incident from around 1943 . . . I was on my way back from somewhere at the time, I remember that even for the climate down there it was really sweltering, and as I was walking across one of the squares in Maksimir, which is a quarter near the centre of town, trucks full of soldiers suddenly appeared from all directions, everyone scarpered but there was nowhere to run and so they rounded up all the people who were there and lined us up against a wall. I was standing all the way to the side of the line and I noticed that directly behind me right above the pavement there was a cellar window, so I got down on my knees and quickly squeezed through — I was thin you know, I was thirteen, maybe fourteen years old — then I ran through the cellar and just as I was crawling out the other side of the building I heard a volley of rifle shots from the town square, the blast was so loud that all the windows in the street shook. But that's not what I wanted to talk about . . . The worst thing was that as I was scampering away I ran past a pile of bricks in the middle of the street with a dead German shepherd on top of it, there's no way it could have got there by accident, it must have been put there on purpose, he'd been shot at close range right here in the head and it looked to me like he was smiling. And only then did I start crying and I ran all the way home. Well, I never told my parents about that . . ."

"Were they Germans?"

"The soldiers? Germans? No, they were Ustashi . . . The Germans were relatively civilised in comparison, but the Ustashi did things no one here would even believe were possible, but after a while you can put things like that out of your mind. Though I'll never forget that dog they'd shot, even now I can see it right before my eyes."

For a while I looked down at the tips of my shoes and Father's shoes, pushing their way through the light and empty air, every now and then kicking away a pebble. I watched the pebbles rolling away. Hitting the curb.

"A friend of mine told me how," I recalled somewhat out of context, "when he was in Russia with a group of climbers somewhere in Tian Shan on a glacier . . ."

"Where?"

"Tian Shan."

"But that hasn't been a part of Russia for a long time, I think it's now part of Kyrgyzstan, it's the upper part of a massif that connects to the Himalayas, then there's the Hindu Kush and in a u-shape above it there's Tian Shan . . ."

"Maybe, but back then it was still part of Russia, damn it!"

"Well, alright then . . . So what happened?"

"Well, walking over the glacier they found a deep crevasse — a chasm — on its upper section and they were struck by an overpowering stench coming from its depths. They thought it was strange, but walked on. And later, below the glacier, they found an underground river that flowed straight out of the ice and the water was so warm they took a swim. While they were messing around down there they found something right by the spot where the river was flowing out, it was wrapped in rags and from a distance you couldn't tell if it was a person or not, and they didn't even bother to find out, they'd had just about enough for one day, the stink up on the glacier and now this . . . Anyway, the next day they reached a mountain hut and there were Russians from the mountain rescue service resting there, talking about how for a week they'd been searching for some family that had got lost in the mountains. So the lads told them about the smell higher up the mountain and the Russians said they'd go up there in the morning but they'd have to show them the spot. They rode there, found the place, and one of the men abseiled down, and as they pulled him up he was all green and said: 'They're all down there, the whole family!' 'How come they smell so bad when it's all ice down there?' the others asked. 'Because of the underground river, their bodies are half submerged in the water, it's a terrible sight I tell you,' the Russian said, 'we'll have to bring a lot of vodka with us when we pull them out.' And then it occurred to Honza, the guy who told me the story, to tell them about the other body they'd found down by the outflow of the underground river. So since they were already up there they went to check it out, and one of the mountain rescue guys went up to it, poked the bundle with a stick, spat, walked back and said: 'That's nothing, just an ordinary goat, let's call it a day and head back!' As they were getting ready to take off, Honza went to take a piss and had one last look at the carcass and only then, looking at it from a different angle, did he notice that the goat was wearing wellingtons . . ."

"Yep, that's Russians for you," Father nodded his head. "One time a guy called Mita joined our lab on a residency and the way he'd kill lab rabbits was he'd grab the animal, stick a pair of rusty scissors in it, snip its artery, grab it by the legs, light a cigarette, and let it bleed to death. When I saw him at it I started shouting but he just stood there staring at me without any comprehension as to why I was upset. And he was a doctor of science, an educated person, but a Russian nonetheless . . . And this friend of yours, he's a mountaineer?"

"No, he's just tried to kill himself in every possible way and still hasn't succeeded."

"Well, anyone who tries hard enough gets there in the end."

"Guess so."

"By the way, the past few days you can see Mars, Jupiter, Saturn, and Venus clearly with the naked eye," Father said, "you know Mars, Jupiter, and Saturn can get quite close to each other, viewed from our perspective that is. They even say that back when Jesus was born it wasn't a comet that appeared but these three planets in conjunction. That must have produced a lot of light in the sky, that's for sure!"

"I guess so," I said, pensively observing the tips of my shoes and the tips of Father's shoes, the pebbles, the tufts of grass poking through the asphalt, the discarded public transport tickets, and then once again the tips of my shoes and the tips of his shoes. *You are out on a walk with your father, it's Thursday afternoon, August, you're alive, this will never be repeated,* a jovial television presenter's voice announced somewhere in my inner self.

"Kozel beer's no longer what it used to be . . . ," Father said.

"I haven't had one in about ten years," I said, "but in any case I'm starting to realise more and more that just about any beer is drinkable as long as it's been well looked after — Smíchov, Benešov, Louny, Krušovice, anything, but there's no beer in existence that carbonation, bad storage, and dirty pipes won't spoil."

"That's probably true," Father retorted, "though Pilsner is Pilsner — could you slow down a little, please? My legs have been giving me trouble lately."

Leisurely, we walked past some crumbling walls. Sheds. Fences. Industrial estates. Cabbage patches. Hedges. Warehouses. Playing fields. Tennis courts. Birches. Larches. Lodging-house buildings.

Two broad-shouldered, sporty-looking young women — fair-haired, uncomplicated athletes with great figures who could easily have decorated the Reichstag — were walking by the fence towards us. At that moment, a loud hooting and yelling came from the lodging house. The curtain parted and two beaming black faces grinned at the blondes. The girls waved at them cheerfully, walked through the gate, and turned into the lodgings. They had firm athletic legs. You could almost hear those colourful drinks and juices advertised on TV swishing about inside them. The hot hearts of cows pulsating inside them. The black guys started to boogie wildly right there in the window: "Yo, yo, yo!"

"What a world . . . ," Father said with resignation.

A bird sang from the copse above the grounds.

"You know what that is?" Father asked.

"What?"

"That bird, the one that's singing?"

"No, I don't," I said vacantly. Right then I was contemplating the huge harpoon in Zeman's film version of Baron Munchausen, the one the size of a cargo plane, which the castaways in the belly of the whale don't notice until it drives through the monster's ribs right next to them. I was thinking that despite being simplistic it's an exact representation of the moment I've been waiting for all my life. The moment when the cataract of routine is ripped and something, *something*, finally happens. I'll be waiting forever, of course. Everyone will. Because everything that does actually happen, immediately takes on the traits of the ordinary. And the brain, that contented brute? That mushy landlord? That aesthete? That Oscar Wilde in my head? It immediately refuses to concern itself with anything new and unknown. Life is driving away under our arses like a bus driven by a stroke-victim, yet the brain is only capable of adding: Oh dear! Well, I never! How curious!

"Oh come on, you can recognise that," Father said, pointing his finger into the copse.

"I don't know," I said vacantly.

"*Chiff chaff chiff chaff,* you must recognise that, *chiff chaff chiff chaff chiff chaff!*" Father yodelled, raising his voice, and one of the sporty babes turned around in surprise.

The fact is, there was a time when he taught me to recognise bird songs. There was a time when we did a lot of walking through the woods together, my unbearable father and I. Novohradské Hills, Jeseníky Mountains, Křivoklátsko, the dry pine forests on the other side of Mělník, the dark spruce forests around Prague, the birch and oak woods near Kladno, the squeaky alder woods along the Berounka River.

"Chiffchaff," I said unwillingly.

"Of course it's a chiffchaff, one of the warblers!"

"Come along then," I said, because I'd realised that we were standing right in the middle of the road, Father because he was listening to a chiffchaff, me because I was trying to take note of some of the crap going through my mind, and in the distance there was a truck coming towards us in a cloud of dust.

We passed the dilapidated old lime works. We crossed over the footbridge above the hollow of disused railway siding. For a while we stared into the gully along whose bottom ran an arc of rusty track, vanishing under dead leaves and branches, a gully dynamite had gnawed into the greasy and crumbly urban crag. *Chiff chaff chiff chaff,* the chiffchaff chirruped from the hill behind our backs.

Cigarettes in hand, we then entered the heart of the Bubeneč district. The space opening before us, framed by graffiti spattered garages, decomposing villas, and brand new used car salons, was called Papírenská Street.

"Aha!" Father said when he noticed the large and intricate brick building we were slowly approaching. Guarded on both sides by two bare chimneys, it was building No. 6, an edifice that looks like a Turkish bathhouse or a sanatorium for eccentric millionaires, or maybe more like an Austro-Hungarian version of the stately Tibetan Potala Palace, but in reality is just a place for processing shit, the former municipal sewage-treatment plant.

When we stood directly in front of the building, Father stopped and examined it for a long time. "Something about it reminds me of Böcklin's *Island of the Dead*," he said quietly.

At that moment the heavy layers of clouds on the distant horizon parted and a red, slimy, flattened sun slipped out between them, looking like it no longer could, or wanted to, stay in one piece. As though it had decided to split in two, four, eight, or tens or hundreds of suns in the next second. White flocks of gulls fluttered above the river.

"Now I remember," Father said, taking off his Prince Heinrich and wiping his forehead while still staring at the shit-treatment plant, "that my mother didn't really want to go back to Bohemia, it was more my father, and they had rows about it . . . She worshipped Tito because he liked raw olives and she did too and he liked to dress in white."

"Tito was a Croat?"

"He was a Croat, but most importantly he was a self-made man, to use the fashionable term. Even my father admired him, he thought Tito was the only person capable of driving the fascists out of the Balkans and he wasn't wrong there, and that's why he joined him, but the problem was he forgot that since the beginning of this world one evil is always driven out by another . . . He believed Tito to be a strong figure, an illusionist, you know, the white elephant. That in his own way he was some kind of peculiar capitalist whose main concern in the end would be prosperity," Father said, his gaze still fixed on the shit-factory, its outline stark against the increasingly dense sky.

"But he still had more class than those Gestapo agents here who later transferred directly to the KGB and moved from the KGB to the government, didn't he?" I said tracking the sun, which suddenly spilled out over the horizon like a broken egg-yolk and then dropped behind the hill. And I saw more clearly than ever before that we are forever enclosed in a grey, impenetrable sphere of smoke, excrement, and laughter. People, the Earth, the Universe and us, the kids. Templates, measures, boxes, and weights. Endless naïvity. Let our language be: yes, yes, no, no. Ha ha.

"What?" Father asked.

"Nothing, what I said was stupid."

"Sorry, I was looking if that isn't a cormorant over there, but it isn't . . . Did Tito have class? Initially I suppose he did, but beginnings never tell you anything about endings . . . There was something else I wanted to tell you, though, every night during the war a Partisan biplane used to fly over Zagreb, probably one of those Russian Polikarpov fighters, but everyone called it the *Smelly Martin*, and every night it dropped a single bomb, probably because it couldn't carry more than one, and of course it never hit anything, the bomb fell somewhere on a meadow or maybe hit a goat shed at best . . . Or is that a cormorant . . . ? But my mother was excited about it, you know, every day she waited by the window for it to fly over, you couldn't miss it because it made a noise just like a sewing machine, and finally once she'd heard an explosion somewhere in the distance she'd say: 'Long live Marshal Tito!' close the window and go to sleep. In fact, I don't think Tito even called himself *marshal* yet, but for my mother he'd already been one for a long time . . . It's my impression that my father took exception on a purely personal basis, that he was basically jealous because my mother worshipped Tito . . . Oh well, it's getting dark, shall we move on?"

We continued the walk, discussing our usual topics along the way. What could possibly be the maximum size of Architeuthis dux and how many of them might be roaming the depths of the oceans; when making a dish of fried wild mushrooms, should you only use one kind of mushroom, Russula, or maybe Armillaria, or is it better to add some Slippery Jacks as well; magic mushrooms are nasty, no point even starting down that road; which one of us was the real hypochondriac.

"I had a mate, his name was Jirka Filek," I started saying, "and for the past ten years whenever we went out for a beer he would always say: 'Don't be stupid, go see a doctor, haemorrhoids are no laughing matter, they'll burst, you'll get blood poisoning and it'll all be over! Go, while there's still time!' and every time he gave me the calling card of some Doctor Nachtigalová who does endoscopy. He was her patient himself at the time, had some trouble with his lungs. In the end I had at least ten of those cards at home. I didn't see Jirka for quite a while and then someone told me he was recovering from an operation, and then I didn't see him again for a few months and then all of a sudden I found a death notice in my mailbox."

"How old was he?" Father asked, somewhat concerned.

"About thirty-five. Recently my stomach's been acting up and . . ."

"You get that after me, I've always had a predisposition for stomach ulcers," Father said.

"I told myself maybe there's no two ways about it, this machine needs an overhaul to be able to lug me around a while longer . . ."

"What machine?"

"This body of mine . . . So I got my shit together and went to see Doctor Nachtigalová. 'Hello, I'm Beneš,' I said, 'you were recommended to me by Jirka Filek, but he died, so I'm not sure it's right to give him as a reference.' 'You knew Jiří?' the doctor said joyfully — by the way she's a real beauty, dark hair, black eyes, and very congenial as well — and straight out she shook my hand. 'Yes I did,' I said. And she offered me a chair and instead of her asking about my ailments we ended up talking about Jirka, recalling all kinds of stories and that sort of thing. I completely forgot why I'd gone there in the first place until the doctor suddenly sighed and said: 'I know, Jiří was a very pleasant person but unfortunately there was no way to save him.' 'I guess he neglected something, eh?' I couldn't help asking. And she said: 'Couldn't really say he'd neglected anything, the metastasis was so rapid that by the time we opened him up it looked like someone had poured acid into his gut, basically he no longer had any intestines left . . .' "

"Well, you know how it is, we're like meat on a counter to

them, what else can they do," Father added in his stride. "So what's wrong with you?"

"Nothing special, she stuck a pipe into my stomach, it made my eyes go red like a rabbit's, and she located some kind of protrusion or something."

"Protrusion?"

"Yeah, some sort of hernia, nothing serious."

"Hold on, nothing serious . . . What kind of hernia?"

"Hiatal."

"Hiatal, okay, but what kind exactly? Axial? Or what?"

"How should I know!"

"I don't get it, you go see a doctor and don't even ask exactly what's wrong with you . . . You taking something for it?"

"Pills."

"What kind of pills?"

"I don't know."

"You don't remember what pills you're taking?"

"Damn it, Dad, we're not in the doctor's waiting room now, I'm telling you all this for a completely different reason!"

"Yeah but this is important . . ."

"Maybe, but we're not going to get to the bottom of it now, I'm telling you a story for Christ's sake!"

"Oh alright, then, tell the story . . ."

"Okay, so seeing as I was already there . . . You know what, it really doesn't matter!"

"Oh come on, I'm listening . . ."

"Okay, so seeing as I was already there at the doctor's," I started recounting with a detached, cracked voice, "I thought it might be a good idea to also ask about these haemerrhoids of mine and she says: 'That's no problem, nowadays we have a standard procedure for outpatients, we simply ligate the affected area and after a while it will fall off on its own. Let's see what you've got to show me . . .' So I took off my trousers, she sprayed the spot with disinfectant, had a look at it and said: 'Oh, well this won't fall off on its own, how long have you had it?' 'Twenty years,' I said. 'This requires an operation, the sooner the better,' the doctor said and very gently tapped the haemerrhoid with her finger, and as she tapped it I got the biggest, most monstrous erection I'd had in a very long time. I stood there sticking out my bum and vainly tried to work out what to do so she wouldn't notice it . . . What an embarrassment!"

"Well well," Father said with a faint smile, "I'm quite envious, with me she could tap just about anything . . . So now what? You going to have the operation?"

"I don't know."

"Hang on, what do you mean you *don't know*, you made an appointment, didn't you!"

"Yeah, right, I will, sometime after the New Year."

"And does it hurt when you, you know . . . ?"

"No, it doesn't hurt."

"Does it bleed?"

"No, it doesn't bleed."

"Hang on, doesn't bleed, is it really a *haemerrhoid* then?" Father bellowed so the entire street could hear and a grimy little man in overalls, who had just walked out of the metal doors of a workshop two metres in front of us, started measuring us up with a curious expression while a pair of cyclists wearing colourful aerodynamic helmets passed us on the other side of the road. The round brown eyes of a brunette in lycra sportswear glared at me for a moment. She seemed to smell of wind.

"Well sometimes it does," I said quietly.

"*Sometimes* it does what?"

"Sometimes it bleeds. Let's not talk about illness anymore," I said.

"It's hard with you, you're always so *tense*. I was only asking, that's all . . ."

Dark Baba Hill appeared looming above the bend of the Vltava, twisted old cherry trees sticking up from its slopes like chicken claws. As we walked, wooden enclosures full of brushwood, sprouting branches, entwined currant bushes and perforated barrels retreated behind us. Sheds painted grey displayed warning signs with pictograms of lightning. Broken insulators.

"You keep thinking that I like to talk about sickness," continued Father, "but when I was bedridden in Thomayer Hospital because of my *leg*, I tried to keep my mind on everything but the hospital because the guy in charge was a Doctor Izmalčov, and let me tell you he didn't mess about. He came to me on the first day, looked at me through his quiff, he had this black quiff hanging down over his eyes, that's their national hairstyle, you know, and says . . ."

"Whose national hairstyle?"

"He was Bulgarian, didn't I say that? A Bulgarian who had studied here and stayed on, he was a really pleasant guy otherwise, but on that first day he says to me: 'Soo, Mister Beneš, this leg of yours is going to be amputated, you know this?' And I got such a terrible fright I couldn't get a word out and just nodded. In the end they managed to bring it back to life and when they were letting me out this Doctor Izmalčov says to me: 'Good-bye, Mister Beneš, so yours leg managed to hang on, I bet you glad! Now you will put on ointment, spare yourself, not walk so much, and I wish you that it functions at least two more years!' So I got a hell of fright again: '*Two years,*' I said, 'and after that?' 'Then we'll get saw out,' said Izmalčov and signed the release form. Well and there you have it, it's been eight years and I'm still walking, I don't hold back, hobbling through the woods and the leg's holding firm! Trust doctors!"

"The only time to see them is when you're at the end of your tether."

"That's right, when my friend Čenda Laburda was fifty-nine he fell in love with a thirty-year-old and decided to have plastic surgery, believe it or not, so that she'd fancy him! I warned him it could have all kinds of side-effects, but Laburda wouldn't listen. Off he went and for an awful lot of money he had his face stretched to smooth out his wrinkles. And in six weeks time he came to see me and was cursing up a storm, saying he used to shave twice a week and now he has to do it *twice a day* because the way they pulled his skin up over his chin he's now got facial hair growing behind his ears. On top of that he's quite dark skinned and even his whiskers are completely white, you know, so there's nothing else he can do, because otherwise he says people stare at him all the time, fact is, he looks like he's got icing sugar all down his neck . . ."

While we were talking we reached the point where Papírenská becomes a normal street. Unexpectedly, two rows of dilapidated apartment blocks rise out of the wilderness of the riverbank, terminating again after about two hundred metres, and then there's only stones and grass. Through the twilit air we were struck by the stench of piss, damp plaster, and mouldy old boots in hallways.

"Well, look at that, I've never been here before in my entire life," Father said surprised, "it doesn't even look like Prague . . . Looks more like a film set for *Dead Eyes of London!*"

"It's a very strange part of town," I said in agreement. "I was walking through here about a month ago and I remembered that one of my friends lives somewhere in these parts and I thought it might be a good idea to ask these three hefty young Gypsies that were hanging around. 'Yeah, sure, a big guy, Franta or Lojza,' they said. 'That won't be him,' I replied, 'this guy's called Pavel,' and they said: 'Oh yeah, yeah, sure, Pavel, big guy, come with us, we'll take you to his place,' and like a complete moron I went with them into the building, out of politeness, you know, so as not to hurt the feelings of somebody who wanted to help me out . . . And straightaway on the ground floor these guys sort of got into formation, one in front of me and two behind, and we went up these narrow winding stairs, looked exactly like we were climbing up the inside of a snail shell. By then I was expecting a knife in the back at any moment. And the first guy suddenly stopped, looked at me and said: 'Aren't you scared?' 'No,' I replied, taking great care to stop my voice from croaking. 'You're not, huh?' he said sort of disappointed, 'okay then, let's go . . .' And when we got upstairs there was a low dark corridor, and he looked at me again and said in disbelief: 'You're still looking for this Lojza, are you?'

'Sure am,' I said, trying to decide if I should attempt to break through the two behind me and make a run for it or ring some-one's doorbell, when one of them started banging on a door and this bloated greasy vampire woman came out wearing a towel around her head and a flowery dressing gown, gold on her ears and around her neck, and the guy said: 'We got someone here looking for that fat Lojza or Franta, you know, big beefy guy . . .' And the hag drew a breath with a loud wheezing sound and started yelling: 'How many times have I told you not to bugger around here! This isn't your building! Your block's over there! Get the hell away from here or I'll get Roman and he'll sort you out, that's for sure! He'll tell you good! And you sir, come right in!' "

"Like she was inviting *you* in?" Father asked.

"I was surprised myself, she was glaring at me with her gold teeth and being all flattering: 'Come in, sir, don't stand out there!' 'I don't want to bother you,' I said, 'I'm just looking for this friend of mine.' And she stopped smiling: 'You're not . . . ? You don't know Roman? You're not bringing us anything?' 'I don't and I'm not,' I said. And she went blue with rage and a drop of saliva appeared in the corner of her lips, I was afraid she might bite me. But that's when a curtain moved in the hallway and this guy walked out from under it, a guy like I'd never seen in my life, head like a hippo's, tiny eyes incredibly far apart, body like the Golem, shoulders, gut, legs — his whole body looked like it'd been enlarged, even the finger that he pointed at me didn't look like a finger but a stick of salami: 'Where's he from?' he asked the hag. 'I don't know, where's he from?' she turned to the Gypsy guys. 'We don't know,' said their leader tamely. 'They don't know,' the hag said submissively. 'What does he want,' asked the man without looking at me. 'He doesn't want anything,' she replied. 'Then he should get out of here,' the giant said and pointed at the Gypsy boss: 'And you get in here.' The guy started shaking and mumbling, but the man pointed at him again and said: 'I'm not going to say it again,' and the guy walked inside and the door slammed behind him. The other two Gypsies were suddenly all crestfallen and said: 'Look, this Lojza probably doesn't live here, so you'd better go.' And as I was running down the stairs, they called to me softly: 'Interested in a cheap cell phone? Or some CDs?' and I was dumb enough to go back up a few stairs to tell them I wasn't."

"Unfortunately that's typical for you," Father nodded.

"What?"

"That you act like you were in a comic book or something."

"I'm just glad when something interesting happens every now and then."

"Something's always happening! Even if you're sitting at home in your comfy armchair, something's always happening! Increasingly sophisticated viruses are continuously trying to reprogram the way your cells work, antibiotics have almost lost their potency, organisms are being cloned, almost every day an animal species disappears from the planet, the darkies have got the atomic bomb, that's not enough for you? Entire nations are being displaced around the world, is that not enough for you?"

"The only thing I'm interested in are people you can sometimes have an interesting conversation with, and there's not many of them left, either. And don't say *darkies!*"

"Yeah, yeah, thank God you haven't seen the kind of filth that surfaces in people in situations when they think it's okay — without a doubt, racism is something we all have in common . . ."

"I don't."

"You don't necessarily have to be aware of it, it only appears under certain conditions. I don't think one person's better than another either . . . All I'm saying is that you don't know what you'll feel until it rears its ugly head again in one form or another. Because all this progress, this humanism of ours, is leading to the point where we'll be smiling apologetically at them while they slit our throats because we're so absolutely certain that *they must have some reason to be upset with us* . . ."

"At who?"

"What?"

"Who are we going to be smiling at?"

"At the darkies, the Arabs, who else . . ."

"Everyone get's their turn, after all, we've wiped out entire nations."

"Who do you mean 'we'?"

"Well, the white race, the white man."

"I've not wiped out any nation, and if you've wiped out some nation at some point then be glad I didn't know about it because I would've given you a good slap. But right now I'm more concerned about the fact that my washing machine's been out of order for over a month and I've no idea where I'll get the money for a new one . . ."

"I don't think anyone's going to be trying to exterminate us," I continued. "More likely they'll just see how much we're willing to put up with and when they find they can get away with just about anything they'll dispose of us like ants of a carcass. And the worst is, they'll basically be doing the right thing . . . You should've said you need a washing machine, we've got a new one now, you could've taken the old one."

"Great, I'll take it!"

"It's gone already."

"Oh, and where on earth did you get the money to buy a washing machine?"

"Hanka bought it."

"Oh right, that's possible."

"Thing is, when I installed it, I didn't bother connecting the outflow pipe, you know that plastic tube at the back, to the drains, I just simply hooked it over the side of the bath tub . . ."

"Ah, I get it, and then you had a bath."

"And the washing machine was washing. I got a little surprise."

"You really can't complain that nothing happens . . . But you're wrong if you think exterminating other nations is the white man's prerogative. Just look at what's been happening over the last two hundred years, the Turks trying to wipe out the Armenians and Kurds, the Indonesians the Timors, the blacks the Arabs and the Arabs the blacks, Stalin, an Asian himself, decimated lots of Asian nations, didn't he, and then there's China, Africa, India, and Pakistan, no point going on. And we're talking about people here, but not even the innocent animals are much better off, although Konrad Lorenz believed animals have an innate mode of behaviour preventing them from wiping out members of their own species en masse, but today we know that's not true. Ants, okay, ants are ants, but even wolves, hyenas, big cats, and many other socially ordered species organise coordinated slaughter of rival groups. And primates? They don't piss about at all, chimpanzees even exterminate entire neighbouring clans, the young and females included, according to a plan, that's regular genocide in every respect . . ."

We walked past a parked black sports car with sharp predatory teeth poking out of the radiator. Canines made from chromium-plated sheet metal twinkled in the light of the streetlamp. For a second I had a feeling that ferocious, preternaturally distended faces were staring at us from the depths of the dark flats, but when I looked around I saw only cracked windows repaired with sticky tape and behind them curtains and flowerpots with cacti.

We reached the last house in the street, walked round it and headed towards the mouth of the pedestrian tunnel leading through the railway viaduct. We entered the piss-saturated darkness. Three metres above our heads a train rumbled, shaking the horsetails growing between the sleepers. When we emerged on the other side we found ourselves surrounded by the hum and buzz of the civilised world, full of lights.

"Ah, but this is Podbabská Street," said Father, cracking his knuckles, "and further on over there that's Yugoslav Partisans Street, where the Švejk pub is, I used to go there every Friday with Alfréd Kahavka. Now *there's* a real alcoholic! You berate me for my drinking, but Alfréd? He's been boozing on a regular basis since he was eighteen, never stopped his entire life, he's sixty-seven now and his mind's working just fine and he's still cheerful, whereas I lived like a monk until I was thirty, I didn't drink at all, and what am I now? A stupid old man . . ."

"Well I'm certainly not berating you for anything."

"Alright, but you were embarrassed of me at your wedding, when you were marrying Blanka, and all I'd done was teach your mother-in-law Croatian, she'd asked me to . . ."

I was shaking my head, but I remembered it very well. Croatian, that wasn't the half of it. I remembered his dancing around the table to amuse the wedding guests, clucking like a hen with his arms above his head, and how initially some tipsy auntie danced with him, but then she sat down and they were all laughing out of obligation. They were looking away because they were a boring bunch of engineers, economists, and teachers, whereas Father, although he was drunk and maybe unbearable in some people's view, in his own mind he thought he was being quietly and discreetly free, as always. And not even I laughed at the time because I have something of my mother in me. Every time after we'd had guests over, the moment they'd left and the door had closed behind them, Mother started to wash the ashtrays with detergent and polish the glass table with window cleaner. She dusted every day. I didn't laugh because I was, and will be, a narrow-minded arsehole.

"Truth is, I was drinking quite a lot at the time," Father continued, "but what can a person do when he has to live in this fucked-up world where you can't find sanity without appropriate local anaesthetic! One way might be to go nuts and then be happy, but I only managed to do that halfway."

"Alfréd's the curly-haired guy who plays the accordion?"

"That's him. The first time he got drunk was with his brother at a ball in Lucerna, he was eighteen at the time, like I said, and since then he's been drinking constantly, it's been forty-nine years already. Most people would be dead by now, but Alfréd? He doesn't even get ill! He doesn't know what a cold is!"

The light was on at a kiosk on the other side of the petrol station. A few sweaty grilled chickens were resting under the glass, showing off their desperate bones in the light of a pink bulb. Behind the counter stood a bloated fellow wearing a red shirt and a white overcoat with a shiny collar. Despite appearances, the wind wafted an appetising odour towards us.

"Are you hungry?" Father asked. *"The best birds I know are geese and ducks, ho ho!"*

"What?"

"You wrote that."

"I didn't write that, that's from some translation of medieval poetry . . . Where do you know it from?"

"You wrote it, you don't even know what you've written anymore, that's my favourite poem . . . Go on, recite one!"

"On the centre court in Prague Štvanice
Whores danced to the sound of a harp
In the moonlit park . . .
I was also there back then
Same as you, Lili Marlen
Playing tennis and drinking gin . . . ," I started immediately.

"Well, there you go, that's an ugly poem if I ever heard one . . . And why Lili Marlen?"

"Hard to say."

"Is that another one you didn't write? Then tell me one you did write."

"Totally fucked up am I with morality," I said.

"Is that it?"

"That's not it, I was just making a dramatic pause."

"Hope so! And?"

"And still the same order clings (inwardly and outwardly) to all things . . ."

"For goodness' sake, what on earth do you mean by *inwardly and outwardly to all things,* I know, you've always liked those sorts of sweeping statements, like something's *one thing* and at the same time its *opposite* . . ."

There was an empty baked-bean tin in the road. I kicked it. It ricocheted away from a cast-iron lamppost and returned back under my feet.

"Well and . . . ? What's the rest of it?" Father said.

I kicked the tin again. Hard. This time it flew into the burdock on the other side of the junction.

"Well, alright . . ." Father sighed, "why don't you tell me what's new in your life?"

"Nothing, just variations on the theme of fish, amphibians, reptiles, and birds."

"Come on, don't be churlish . . . You never know, this might be our last walk together, tomorrow I might kick the bucket and we won't see each other ever again. You hungry? I'll get you a chicken."

"No thanks."

Car breaks screeched a few metres away from us. A few adolescent mutants looking for mischief jumped out of a Nissan suv covered in colourful stickers and surrounded the kiosk. "Buy all the chicken they've got . . . !" yelled their companions from the car, sixteen-year-old chicks with bob haircuts, deep-cleansed foreheads and faces plastered with make-up, "hahaha . . . , whoopeee, get some chicken. . . and coke . . . and sprite . . . rye rolls . . . and some menthols . . . ! Something sweet . . . ! Something salty . . . ! Something with strawberries . . . !"

Bam bam bam, boom boom boom came the music.

"Blondes have definitely been massively on the increase over the last thirty years," Father said incredulously, "didn't used to be like this, today there are blonde girls all over the place . . . Maybe it's the diet or something . . ."

In the meantime the teenagers were competing to see who could throw a piece of chicken the farthest. A slick-haired scraggy guy with a slightly hunched back tossed the chicken as far as the bushes below the embankment. The shapeless fatso with peroxide hair would certainly have thrown further but the chicken piece hit a makeshift cable and crashed into a greasy puddle behind the petrol station. The man behind the counter looked on, a match in the corner of his lips. "Coooooool!" the girls squealed. Then the guys threw the bag with the rest of the chicken on the seat, got in the car and drove off.

"I've been saying to myself a long time now that one of the few dignified forms of employment in this world is to be a hired killer, too bad I didn't take it up when I was young," Father said, "I don't mean in relation to this lot, a hired killer has to be free of all emotions and that's what's nice about it . . . You sure you don't want any chicken?"

"No, really," I said.

"Oh go on, have some, you've got to eat . . ."

"I've eaten."

"What did you eat?"

"Doesn't matter."

"But you can tell me, can't you?"

"Well, I made myself a beef patty, a *karbanátek*."

"*One* karbanátek?"

"Four."

"How do you make them?"

"I take minced beef, mix it with some dry white bread that's been soaked in milk, add some coarsely chopped onion, a clove of garlic is optional, an egg, salt and pepper, crumbled dried thyme, sometimes a bit of dill . . ."

"Dill?"

"Sounds strange, but it's not bad. Well, and then I just coat them in flour, put them in a pan and fry."

"That could be tasty, but you don't coat them in breadcrumbs?"

"No."

"Why not, it's just that technically speaking it's not a real *karbanátek* if you don't coat it with breadcrumbs . . ."

"Hmm."

"I just hope you'd say so if you felt like having some chicken . . ."

"Come on, I weigh almost a hundred kilos again, why do you keep on . . . You have some!"

"Me? Might as well eat shards of glass. With my diet I can't have chicken at all, those days are over when I could cook myself goulash with a kilo and a half of lean shin of beef, of course lower shank is better, but where can you get that nowadays . . . and no bacon fat or oil to start with, just pure lard, oh yes, simmer and add a green pepper and two or three tomatoes at the end . . . ," jabbered away one of two figures, pitter-pattering together along the asphalt-covered bottom of the world. The one wearing a light white raincoat billowing in the wind gesticulated sharply with his hands and walked with a wide gait as though suffering from leg pains. The other, wearing a shirt and baggy trousers, was holding a satchel firmly under the arm, looking around, shaking its head and shrugging its shoulders. From a height it was not possible to see their faces. From even higher up they just looked like schematically carved wooden figures, jerkily moving along the periphery of a fractured nativity scene at night. Like the puppets Jů and Hele at the bottom of a dried-up aquarium. And from further up you couldn't even make out anything, only the dark strip of the river heading out of the pulsating city between jetties and locks, meandering in a wide sweep.

We headed back in the direction of town along the empty, mon-umentally wide boulevard built in the fifties. After a while we walked past a drinking hole by the name of Eufrat that's never been known by any other name than Arafat. Viewed through the window, the green neon announcing that Staropramen beer cir-culated in its pipes hopelessly flickered and hummed. We walked back and looked inside. The punters sat hunched over the tables, staring ahead, biting into brawn and drinking beer.

"Dear me," Father said quietly, "shall we look for another place?"

"We could have one to quench the thirst and then move on."

"That's an option."

We sat at the back and watched the horizontal layers of smoke shrouding the bar. After a while I took my diary out of my bag, looked up a number, and popped out to make a call. When I came back, two beers stood on the table and Father was writing a note in my diary.

Bikst: lambda/3x (Gik Gst-Gis Gkt), I read.

"What's that?" I asked.

"That's the Riemann-Christoffel curvature tensor for the radius of the universe," he said.

"And what am I supposed to do with it?"

"You? Nothing, have another vodka."

"I'd better not," I said, because I'd noticed that the pub was swaying a little, "but maybe I could have a Jarošek juniper-berry brandy. That's not bad."

"That's not at all bad . . . have they got it? I'll have one as well, but tell me, seeing as you're still buying *Aviation*, do you think we're going to end up buying those Grippens or not?"

"Probably will because I'd say that someone's already been paid off and they're just waiting for a while so it's not so blatantly obvious."

"Well actually, I'm glad about that, I really like the Grippen, I already liked the Vigen and the Draken and even the Lansen, all the jets built by SAAB with the exception of the Tunnan, I'm sure you like that one . . . I wonder if you know what *tunnan* means in Swedish?!"

"Barrel . . . To me it looks like a squeeze toy."

"The Grippen?"

"That's right."

"And what don't you like about it?!"

"That it's like a light sporty plane, like a little monkey on a rubber band, a spoilt princess. A little moth."

"I understand, the only plane for you is the Su-35, oh well, you can't stop progress . . . And technological progress has a feedback influence on people's view of what they like or don't like, even of what they think is and isn't possible . . . Back in 1903, though this is going to make you lose your temper and say I'm pontificating again, the renowned and highly regarded astronomer Newcomb published a work in which he proved that no airplane heavier than air could fly, because it's against the laws of physics, well, and in December of that same year the Wright brothers flew for the first time, didn't they . . . And no later than the middle of this century, pilotless planes will be quite common and they'll just be these boring pancake-like composites packed with electronics, you won't like them at all, even though you luckily won't live to see them," Father said. "Listen, on a different note, you're not drinking too much, I hope?"

"Not too much," I said.

"Don't take me as an example, though I didn't start until after I'd finished my studies. I didn't touch a drop until I was thirty! Though it's true that every thirst is the result of yesterday's thirst, as Švejk says, and a normal person can't get out of it that easily, it's like the story of the cabinet-maker who got drunk for the first time in his life on New Year's Eve and on January 1 he was so thirsty and felt so sick he bought some pickled herrings and started drinking again, and no one could help him because every Saturday he always bought a week's supply of pickled herrings . . ."

We clinked glasses of Jarošek juniper-berry brandy.

"Aaaah," was the noise Father made.

"Aaaah," was the noise I made.

"But what I can't get into my head are those women of yours," he began as usual.

What about your women . . . erupted in my head as though a gas pipe had burst: What about that crazy Marcela . . . ! What about the done-up fashion model, the one with the tits that gave anyone she met a big slobbery kiss, what about the sleepy mousy one with highlights . . . ! The one from Vrchlabí . . . ! What about that Jonáková, I wouldn't touch her with a bargepole . . . ! And what about my mother, after all . . . ! And don't quote Švejk . . . ! You frittered away our house . . . ! Where's all that money . . . !? roared inside my head. As always.

"Okay, leave the women out," I said.

"Why? I quite liked Renata, for example, what really fascinated me about her was that she could piss in a sink like a man, unless you made that up, of course . . . But the others, well, I suppose there was the small one with the big tits, at least she was solid, but that Michala, she was a complete loon, wasn't she, though I guess she was quite pretty, but that other ex of yours, Rezeda, not even worth talking about. Although you have made some progress in your relationships, that's for sure, but you'll be fifty soon. What about this Hanka?"

"She's the best woman I've ever met, now you mention it, although sometimes I get the feeling that I definitely don't deserve her."

"Well you're right there . . . I commend you for that . . . Are you going to get married?"

"Probably not, but Hana's going to be thirty in a year so there'll have to be a baby."

"Hope it's not too late!"

"I should still be able to squeeze out a drop or two."

"You know the longer you wait the higher the risk that something might go wrong . . ."

"All kinds of things can happen . . . Once, conjoined twins, Johan and Lazarus Batista Kolledero, were born in London and they were formed in such a way that Johan was growing out of the chest of his normally developed brother, so throughout their lives they were looking at each other's faces. Johan was only functional in his own right from the waist up, like he'd been grafted onto his brother. The problem was that they had different personalities. Lazarus was a cheerful sort, he liked company and liked to have a drink, whereas Johan didn't drink at all, in fact he didn't even eat and was an introvert by nature. So people were always inviting Lazarus out and liked him, whereas Johan had the reputation of a parasite standing in the way of his brother's happiness, and that led to Johan's becoming jealous of his brother. He started to throw reproachful tantrums and no longer wanted to go out and socialise, he wanted to sit at home and maybe take walks in the garden, if that. But Lazarus was the one with the legs so Johan had to go from one party to another against his will. Apparently they always argued about it, and Johan would end up offended, staring at the ceiling all night, while Lazarus would fool around, tell jokes, and in between he'd reason with his brother in a quiet, friendly voice . . ."

"Oh right, so how are things with Hanka, then? I don't mean it in a bad way, I'm your father, that's all, so I just don't want you to mess things up in your life the way I did, I'm terrified to see that you take after me . . . You're not here only for yourself, you know!"

"And for what, then?"

"Reproduction, that's what!"

"I don't suffer from any exaggerated desire to reproduce my genes, although I've already slipped-up once . . ."

"What do you mean, 'slipped-up'?"

"Oh, you don't know about this yet. I only found out myself a year ago," I said because it was too late to back out.

"Well I wonder what I'm going to find out now . . ."

"To keep it brief, right after I'd done my time in the army I went out with this girl called Martina . . ."

"You mean tiny Zuzana? The one with the littlest hands who was always brushing her hair?"

"No, I said it happened with *Martina*, right after I got out of

67

the army! And Martina came up to me back then and said she was expecting a child and she'd like me to know straight out that it's not mine, though she wanted me to know that even so she still loved me. So we stayed together for a while longer and then it was over, not because of the child, there were other women involved, you know, I was twenty at the time, she was a few years older and she was seeing some other guys as well . . ."

"For Christ's sake . . ."

"Yeah. And last summer by pure coincidence I ran into Martina and we went for a coffee together and when we'd drunk two litres of wine she suddenly started crying: 'There's something I have to tell you, the boy I had, he's yours, I kept it from you because I didn't want to cause you, and especially myself, any trouble. I knew that with your personality you'd have to do a lot to deal with it and even then it wouldn't work out . . .' 'Okay,' I said, 'but now you've told me, I'd like to see him, at least once.' 'Well, okay, but there's two problems, for one I don't live in Prague and for another I don't want you to introduce yourself as his father, although he knows the guy who lives with us isn't his father. I don't want things more complicated for him than they need to be . . .' "

"I can certainly see what she was getting at," Father noted.

"So I went to Poříčany where they live. Thing is, every Friday she goes to a café on the square and every time her son drops by to borrow a couple hundred crowns on his way from his rehearsal because he wants to be able to make an impression on the girls. So we made a plan for me to be sitting there as though we'd run into each other by accident."

"Oh . . . What rehearsal?"

"He plays in some band. So I went there and we were sitting

in the café, talking. At half past eight in the evening Martina says: 'Hey, don't get upset, but he's probably not going to turn up, it hasn't happened in a long time that he hasn't shown, I guess it's just bad luck on your part.' 'Never mind,' I said, 'at least we had a chance to chat and I guess I'll be on my way.' And the moment I finished the sentence, the doors opened and there stood this unpleasant-looking, obviously hypersensitive, scrawny guy, five earrings in each ear and sporting a goatee, and he made his way over to our table. The blood froze in my veins and my heart started pumping like it was trying to jump out of my body because the person I saw in front of me was me twenty years ago, a confused, essentially negative, hypersensitive shit who views the world as an incomprehensible maze of emotions. In short, I saw an exact copy of the mess I had been at his age . . ."

"Oh well," Father said, "oh well . . ."

"And then he stumbled over to the table, took the money from his mum, looked me over indifferently and was about to take off. 'Sit down with us for a bit,' Martina said to him. 'And what would I talk to you about?' he said, and he was right. I was clutching my mug of coffee, incapable of getting a single word out, and maybe for the first time in my life I felt like I was going to faint big time. And as the boy was closing the door behind him, I noticed he had Killing Joke written on the back of his jacket."

"And this is all true, is it?" Father asked distrustfully.

It was. I'd only changed the name of the woman in question and the name of the place, because on several occasions in the past giving precise geographical details hadn't paid off.

"That was the last time you saw him?"

"We agreed that she wouldn't tell him anything unless he

asked himself. He stayed on my mind, it'd be a lie for me to say he didn't, but what was I supposed to do after twenty years . . . About half a year later, in other words not long ago, I was at home walking around in my T-shirt listening to some music when the doorbell suddenly rang and there he was in the doorway, chewing gum and saying: 'Hey . . . I was talking to my mother and she told me, you know . . . hey, it's no big deal, I'll be on my way again, no problem, no hassles, it's just that I happened to be walking by and, you know, tried ringing the doorbell, you know . . .' 'Come in,' I said, feeling like fainting again because it was daylight and on top of that there was his voice. I felt like I was in some kind of time warp and the person I was talking to in the hallway was myself. We sat down and talked, mostly about some girl who was giving him trouble, how she wants him and then she doesn't. And between sentences he asked me if I had anything to eat, that he hadn't eaten all day, so I showed him the fridge and said he could just take whatever he wanted . . ."

"Okay, I get it," mewled Father.

"What?"

"He wanted money, didn't he?"

"Not at all! The reason I'm saying this is because as he was rummaging through the fridge, I was putting some water on for coffee and even though I'd never brought up any kid in my life I suddenly heard myself — to my great surprise — saying very loudly: 'Don't eat that sausage cold, you know what kind of shit they make them out of? There's a sauce pan over there, heat it up! For God's sake, put it on a plate at least!' "

"Alright, so what are you going to do next?"

"We've gone out for a beer together a couple times so far and it looks like we'll go on doing that."

"And Hanka knows about it?!"

"Of course, it's no big deal. He's an adult lout and so am I."

"And what's his name?" Father asked.

"Robert."

"Aha . . . Well, it's your life in the end, but a man should look after his kids, you know that much I guess."

"And how was I supposed to do that when I've known for less than a year?!"

"I mean in general, in the end I'm glad you're like me and not like your mother, she was an absolute puritan, I always had to get her tipsy for her to let me even touch her, before we got married we'd only had sex three times or so, after all, you were probably conceived on the third go . . . Otherwise I loved your mother, no doubt about that, but it wasn't easy."

"I loved her too. Anyway, at least I tried. But it's strange, the year she died I kept having this frightening, vivid dream where I'm sitting at Mother's on a visit, she's silent, smoking a BT cigarette and looking out the window, a cherry tree is rustling in the wind and in the distance trucks are rolling down the motorway. I'm looking at her and realise that I don't feel a thing, not a thing, no compassion, no remorse, no anger, simply no form of closeness whatsoever. In the end I light up as well and the thought runs through my head: *Why did I have to be born into such a desert!*"

"Desert?"

"That's what I say to myself in the dream. And then when I'm about to flick the ash from my cigarette, Mother says: 'Not there! I just cleaned that one, take the Bulgarian ashtray that's in the kitchen!' And I'm looking at her, trying to feel something human, but all I can see in front of me is the way that for all those years the dusting and vacuuming was done, a whole life cleaning and watching that actress Janžurová in those serials *The Ambulance*, and *The Cottagers*, and *Conversations with Horníček*, instead of living just a little. So I grab the ashtray and smash her over the head with it. She falls down so lightly, like she was made of foam or something. And I'm sitting there, lighting one cigarette from another, and Mother's lying on the floor as I flick my ash onto the carpet."

"Well that's very nice, that is."

"Yeah, and seeing as I'm stupid enough to tell you something like this, I might as well finish. This dream kept recurring, the same thing every time, every time I whack her as if against my will, and then at night I put her in the car and drive her someplace and bury her in this little wood in Krejcárek. And as if that weren't enough, I keep going back there to have a look, not that I want to, I can't help myself. I keep walking around the place, scared stiff, until finally every time I go right to the place, kneel down and start digging and digging until I'm sure the body's still there . . ."

"That's pretty heavy stuff, not very nice at all. I just hope it wasn't caused by some trauma during your childhood, you didn't have a *bad* time in Buštěhrad did you, or did you? I'd honestly feel really bad if that was the case . . ."

"I can't complain about my childhood, that was okay," I heard a forty-four-year-old son say to a seventy-one-year-old father, "that Pepík Mother married was basically a nice guy."

"I never got to know him. When I drove up to see you on the weekends, he hid from me, every single time, or at least that was my impression."

"That's possible. He was a little insecure about himself in his own way but I don't think he was a bad bloke. Fact is though, he was essentially a pleb with a complex and on top of that he was a brass hat. Thinking back, I also suspect he was with the secret police, though I don't think he was a complete bastard . . ."

"The way you talk it sounds like you didn't know him, you guys lived together for how long, twelve years?"

"But I just couldn't stand him. He did everything according to schedule. He was forever spouting these army slogans from the barracks and just wouldn't let up. *'Pleasure No. 1: when you finally take off shoes that are too tight having worn them all day! Pleasure No. 2: when you've been desperate for a dump for a long time and finally take it! The machine gun is your friend! All clear on the right, tanks on the left! To think means not to know shit!'* — that was him all over. He was like a character from some social-realist novel about progress, the son of a miner and a servant girl, an only child, a notable personage in his village with a career in the army, holidays in Burgas, living a fucked-up little Bolshevik life, subconsciously trying to fuck up the lives of everyone else around him. Half his relatives had cushy jobs in military administration, the ministries, the president's office . . . But when I look back, I sometimes regret not having behaved at least a little better towards him. He must have had hell with Mother, because all those years she'd let him know on a daily basis he was a neanderthal, which he was, but not even he deserved to be humiliated. With hindsight I'm not surprised he eventually ran away from her. I don't think he was really angry at her or anything, he just couldn't take it anymore . . . Maybe he was a bastard, what do I know. I didn't really know him."

"I wasn't cross with your mother either, she just wanted to do well for herself and when she saw what it meant to live with the son of a factory owner under Communism, I guess she just reassessed the situation and married a Communist. Back then she told me frankly she wasn't going to swim against the tide. Oh well, never mind, that was a long time ago . . ."

"Exactly," I said.

And the grimy ATM of my mind served up a memory. I'm lying in my bed in the morning, I can't be any older than five, when the door opens and immediately they are standing over me, my black-eyed father Ivan with the protruding ears, a research scientist by profession, and my blue-eyed mother Zdena, her hair curled, a secretary by profession. They are standing over me, uttering a sentence they'd obviously prepared in advance: "Honzí, listen, if we moved away from Klánovice, which one of us would you like to stay with . . . Daddy or Mummy?" "Mummy," I answered stubbornly, because the day before I'd gotten a spanking from my dad for biting his finger. He'd made me a fairly decent battleship from wooden sticks and spatulas but it was only equipped with eight cannons so I was forced to insist their number be increased. I demanded that it should bristle with guns. He felt eight were enough. I swallowed my sense of injustice and then a few hours later, pretending it was in the heat of the moment entirely unrelated to the battleship incident, I bit him. I was a sulky little rat temporarily in the position of an only child. "With Mother," I answered stubbornly. And that was that.

"And what about that Pepík, he still alive?" Father asked.

"He died last year on Christmas Eve," I said.

"Oh, how old was he? I think he was a bit younger than me . . . What did he died of?"

"The story goes that on the afternoon of Christmas Eve he was sitting in the living room in Buštěhrad with the woman he'd left Mother for. They were drinking coffee, the salad was ready, the tree was decorated, the presents were laid out, when Pepík suddenly said: 'You hear that? Someone's calling me, I'm going to take a look outside!' and the woman said: 'Who'd be calling you? Martínek rang the doorbell this morning, it works, they'd ring wouldn't they?' But after a while he pricked up his ears again: 'I can't help it, someone's calling me, I can hear *Pepík!*' and the woman said: 'Why would someone be calling you, that's nonsense, just stay put!' And Pepík said: 'Can't you hear it? *Pepík!* And again: *Pepík!* I'm going to go take a look . . .' He walked out and didn't come back for a long time. When the old girl went to look for him half an hour later, he was lying on the lawn in the snow right by the door, staring at the sky, dead."

"So what did he die of then?"

"Heart failure, one, two and that was it, his pump burst."

"Well, that's a good way to go."

"That it is."

"Uncle Fredy passed away in a similar fashion, you know, your mother's brother, a fine fellow, I liked him best out of all the relatives . . . Every time we'd visit them he'd tell the women we were going fishing and then we'd do the rounds in Kopřivnice, calling on his various acquaintances, drinking with them, and before dawn we'd walk up into the hills, even if it was raining, we'd walk. And Fredy would be giving me the details of where and how he'd shagged some dame again. He'd always say: 'I'm not boring you am I, Ivan? Though even if I were boring you, I'd have to tell you anyway because you're the only person I can tell around here!' One time we were in a flat where everyone was drunk and there was this one extremely beautiful woman there who'd been married off the week before, and her husband was there and lots of relatives. When the party was in full swing, Fredy whispers to me: 'Ivan, you've got to entertain them now for at least half an hour!' So I put a lampshade on my head, painted my face yellow, put on a red dressing gown, and told them I was going to cook a proper Chinese meal for them and asked if they'd like some. They started yelling: 'Sure, get cooking! We'll eat anything! We'd even eat tuna fish!' so I diced everything I could get my hands on, started frying it in the pan, every now and then I poured some liquor on it and flambéed it all for a bit of fun so they wouldn't get bored, you know, it was a lot of laughs . . ." Father said, taking a swig of his beer.

"And where was Uncle?"

"I didn't know that either. I was terrified they'd notice he was gone and so was the bride, but they just kept laughing and shouting: 'I can't believe it! Look at him! I can't believe it!' And Fredy? In the morning up in the hills all misty-eyed he thanked me, saying it was the best screw of his life, because he was with her the whole time in a fancy room next door and the bride, because she was petrified someone might walk in, apparently did things that a decent woman would be too embarrassed to even think about . . . I never did find out how he did it, bald from an early age with a crooked nose, but women had the hots for him to such a degree that over the years he probably managed to fuck every woman in Kopřivnice. He had so many stories, he couldn't tell them all even if he had a whole week. A few times during the summer just the two of us would walk along the river, sleeping wherever we got the urge, and every day we'd stuff ourselves so full of trout we almost burst . . . Damn it, what a shame! Let's have one more Jarošek!" Father said, and I got the impression he'd gone a little misty-eyed.

"Didn't he die while fishing?" I said.

"That's right, he went fishing and never came back, heart failure as well. He should have been lying in hospital but instead he went out to fish for eels, a pig-headed Moravian Valach he was . . . Well, you see I was always sure there's nothing after death, that the energy that is the cause of our perceiving everything as *matter* just simply goes off and serves elsewhere. But recently I've had some strong doubts and it's my impression that there is something more, although I don't see a single sensible reason why that should be so. The thing is, sometimes I get the jitters imagining that there will *never be anything anymore* . . . I guess I'm going senile."

"Well, I've had four or five experiences," I said with care, "that I can't explain in any other way than that there is something on the other side, maybe just some transfer turnstile from where something transmits for a while before it completely disappears or moves away."

"Tell me about it, that's interesting."

"There's the day your father died, for instance. I woke up with a feeling that's very hard to describe. When I opened my eyes I was lying down and unable to move properly, just had the jitters. I felt like I'd been buried by an avalanche. I had no idea what was going on. So I waited until everyone was gone, I didn't bother going to school, I stayed in bed, shaking until evening. The door slammed in the evening, Mother walked into the room, came over to me and said: 'Honza, I have to tell you something, this morning . . .' but she didn't finish because when she saw me she went all pale and ran off crying to the bathroom. To this day I'm not sure what she saw. And I didn't have the slightest idea Granddad was ill or that he was in the hospital . . ."

"There was an incredible connection between you two, he was always talking about you, every day, all those years. Who knows, maybe when his time came he was thinking about you, in fact it's almost certain. Oh well . . . And the other one?"

"Then there was the case of this neighbour of mine who burnt to death, burnt right through my door into my kitchen."

"You told me that one already but I can't believe it, not that I suspect you of making the *whole* thing up but you were on some *substances* at the time, weren't you?"

"Why can't you ever just take it the way I say it?"

"Well, because I know you."

"Alright," I said, "we don't have to talk about anything then!"

"Why shouldn't we, don't get offended straight out . . . That's two, what about the third case?"

"Oh, a friend of mine summoned up a spirit in '88."

"It wasn't the spirit she'd been drinking, was it? Okay, sorry, only joking . . . And what about this spirit?"

Fuck it . . . the demon in my head mumbled: Fuck, fuck,

fuck . . . ! Shit and bugger . . . ! I don't have time for this crap . . . !

"What about the spirit? It was a ghost, that's all!" I was saying vacantly into my beer.

"And what about it?"

"To cut it short, there were about six of us at this girl's cottage, I was going out with Zuzana back then . . ."

"Ah, finally! The little one, the one with the tiniest hands!"

"And this girl I knew, Natasha, came up with the idea to invoke spirits before midnight. She used to say it ran in her family, which sounded quite probable once you'd seen her family: her father was a doddery upper-crust alcoholic, her mother a 100-kilo Russian, and her brother an effeminate epileptic who tried to behave like an old-fashioned aristocrat and musketeer — his walls were decorated with swords and he dreamt of dying in a duel but that couldn't happen because he sat at home all the time drinking apple juice and reading Rimbaud . . . So we were sitting upstairs in this little room in the attic around a table and Natasha started summoning . . ."

"How?"

"She had a big board with numbers and the alphabet in a circle round the perimeter. And all of us fools who were taking part just had the tips of our fingers on a plate that oddly enough actually moved around, pointing to different letters."

"How could a *plate* point to *letters?*"

"There was a pointer on it. But the thing was that twice it didn't make any sense because Natasha just managed to summon some idiot who kept writing UREIT, UREIT, UREIT round and round . . . But because it was at night and there was nothing to drink we kept at it. Natasha suddenly asked if anyone wanted to call on someone they once knew, and right away we all became

sombre, and the thought of *what if* just seemed to hang in the air
. . . Then Zuzana, who always went straight to the point, said
she'd like to talk to Jandourek, who was this sullen sort of guy
who had fallen pathologically in love with her and kept trying to
convince her that they were born for each other and she didn't
have the right to resist it, and when she finally broke up with him
and started going out with me he would call her at three in the
morning and not say anything when she picked up the phone,
just keeping silent. He sent her letters, waited for her in the
metro for hours at the transfer station so that if they ran into
each other he could walk off tragically without uttering a word
and that sort of thing. And in the end he drowned in the Vltava."

"In the Vltava?"

"There was a bunch of them walking over Legií Bridge, he got
up on the railing and walked along it, and because he'd had a few
he took a wrong step and fell into the water. But then he even
shouted at them that he was okay and they should wait for him
on the bank, he'd swim over. They didn't find him until two
months later. He was stuck down under the weir where the Expo
58 Pavilion used to be, next to that power station on Štvanice
Island . . ."

"Right. And did he talk to you guys?"

"We thought he wouldn't want to, he was that sort of guy
even when he was alive, the scornful type, proud, pallid, patron-
ising. Nonetheless, Natasha articulated something along the lines
of our wanting to speak to this Jandourek. For a long time nothing happened. And then suddenly the room became strangely
damp, unwelcoming, like when the door flies open at night letting
in the cold, and then the plate started moving . . ."

"For goodness' sake!" Father said.

"So . . . back to Zuzana, all she did was exhale like a punctured tire, she went pale and took her hands away. After a while the others gave up as well until the only people left with their fingers on the plate were me and Natasha. And the plate glided around, chattering away. How does she do it, I kept wondering that whole evening, how can a dainty girl like that pull a plate around with the tips of her fingers and make it spell out letters like that? It was just the two of us with our fingers on it and it was sliding over the table like greased lightning. I admit that a dry terror suddenly passed through me at that point . . . 'Spirit . . .' Natasha mumbled with a strange croaky voice, and it was clear that even she was scared, 'spirit, would you like to talk to us? Is there any person at the table that you don't approve of?' And before she could finish the plate sort of started rattling, and then I saw that even Natasha had moved her hands away and I was the only one with my fingers on it! And before I could let go the plate started to move towards me — I was pushing it *away from me* — but it slid under my hands, jumped over the edge of the table, leapt into my lap, fell on the floor, and broke."

"Sounds like you've been describing something from an old scratched movie. And what did the little one do?"

"Not a lot, she was . . . You know what? I don't know. I can't remember if she ran away or sat there, but I remember she cried the rest of the night, in a noble sort of way, sitting in the armchair, looking ahead, letting the tears flow down her cheeks like Anna Karenina."

"That must have been becoming."

"It was."

"Oh well. And the other incident?"

"That was when Marie died, one of my friends. For a few days after I had the sensation that she was standing in the corner, trying to tell me something, but I couldn't understand a thing because she was talking in Viennese German, *oooaaaoooaaaoaoooa*, she came from Vienna. And that's all, come on, let's have another juniper brandy . . ."

I preferred not to say anything about the cottage in Šumava where at night the door would softly and mysteriously open on its own, even though it normally scraped the floor. I would have gotten an earful for that. Or about the time in the same cottage when my teeth started aching and for that reason I didn't go with the others to the dance in Stachy, the village down the hill. Well they didn't actually hurt that bad, but I said they did because I didn't want to go to the stupid village dance — no way was I going to tell him about what happened that time. How I'd locked myself in good and proper because they were going to stay in Stachy till the next day, which made sense since it was four kilometres uphill through the woods to get back. How I'd chopped up wood in the vestibule to have enough to put on the fire and the way I exuberantly drove the axe into the chopping block and went to sleep. How I woke up after a night of heavy poisonous dreams and went to chop some more wood to keep the fire going. How I found the axe far away from the chopping block, lying on the floor at the other end of the five-metre long vestibule, where it couldn't have gotten on its own by any stretch of the imagination. How I thought maybe some drunken fool had broken in during the night. How I went to check the doors, but the doors were locked and bolted with a strong oak latch from the inside, ha! I wouldn't tell Father about that in a million years! That would get his head shaking vigorously! Looking out the window! Making demonstrative pauses! Interjections!

"Oh well," Father said, "but most likely those are all phenomena of this world, besides the fact that even the memory you have of something that you think happened with one hundred percent certainty isn't reliable . . . The thing is, the brain has to *recreate it all* when you want to recall something, and the stuff it's making it from may not be authentic, and often it isn't. You don't know if you hadn't by chance seen it in a film, or maybe you heard it or read it somewhere, and who knows, maybe some kinds of memory can even be *inherited* . . . All those so-called primitive nations are dead right in not distinguishing between dreams and reality, it's all much more interwoven than we'd like, and then it's hard to tell . . . When you were still riding around in your baby carriage we had a bullterrier called Baryk, he used to crawl right into your carriage with you, he was such a kind and amiable dog, but your mother was afraid he was going to maul you and she insisted we get rid of him, so my father gave him away, and I would have sworn that dog was grey-white, slightly on the darker side, and that he had two spots right there, and that's how I remembered it for many years . . . And recently I found an old photograph with Baryk in it and he was all white!"

"I remember that dog," I said.

"You can't remember him . . ."

"I remember how someone was licking my gob with a wet tongue when I was lying in the carriage, must have been him. And the way that pine trees swayed high above me."

"That's strange, it must have been Baryk because no one else back then licked your face, except maybe Mrs. Truhlářová, she had a habit of kissing you . . ."

"But she scratched because she had stubble, whereas this was pleasant. And I also remember I was so angry when the dog was taken away I ate chicken shit, but that's a bit hazy. I know I ate chicken shit because for one I remember Mother repeatedly telling me not to do it, and to this day I remember what it tastes like."

"And what does it taste like?"

"It's got a sort of caustic, bitter tang, somehow death-like, I've never tasted anything as morbid since."

I took a swig and realised Father was staring with a terrified expression at something in one corner of the room. I looked in that direction. There was a bunch of grown-up kids, their hair already going grey, lowering shots of green mint liqueur into freshly drawn pints of beer. The shots descended to the bottom of their mugs like small, heavy divers.

"Oh Christ . . . ," Father said slowly.

"What's the matter?" I asked.

"Will you look at that, what are they doing . . ."

"They're drinking a Magic Eye."

"*Logic* Eye?"

"Magic. Don't you know it?"

"No I don't, where could I have come across such an abomination? It's not something you actually drink, is it?"

"Of course, it's a classic cocktail, an essential part of the repertoire. We've been drinking it in Žižkov since I can remember."

"Well that's very nice, that is . . ."

"It's a nasty drink, though I find it hard to believe you've never seen one before."

"I've seen all kinds of things, but I'm sure I'd remember this sort of barbarity . . ."

"You remind me of a landlady from a pub in Bořivojova Street. In 1990 they opened this brand new place there on the corner where there'd always been a pub, but suddenly there were American flags everywhere, new tables and new staff . . ."

"And what about this landlady?"

"She was just like you. When we tried ordering Magic Eyes — we were feeling nostalgic — she had no idea what we wanted. A landlady! So we ordered beer and mint liqueur separately and when we dropped the shots into the beer glasses, this beast of a woman rushed over and started screaming: 'I'm not having that in my establishment, you can do it anywhere else you like but not here! I'm not serving you another drink! Pay up and go!' We sat there staring at her and just couldn't think of anything to say, so we paid and left."

"I've tried a cocktail or two in my time, of course, every now and then, you know — Sabres & Swords, otherwise known as Mother & Father, that was rum and cherry liqueur," Father said, rubbing his chin.

"We knew that as a Red Hammer, but you had to add fruit wine and maybe a drop of Francovka liniment."

"When you're young you can survive almost anything . . . I also remember Gypsy in the Grass — that was really foul . . ."

"Devil in Stromovka, mint liqueur and Fernet, that's a classic layered drink, of course. When you add rum it's called Journey into Prehistory . . ."

"And that's nothing compared to what's known as a Brain, the only person who could drink that was Alfréd Kahavka, he used it to pick up women, I hope you don't know that one?"

"Sure do, advocaat and cherry liqueur, something dreadful."

"Disgusting, definitely . . . Then there's Beton, of course, Becherovka and tonic, and the Bavarian, Fernet and tonic, I quite like that, and then there's vodka with champagne, otherwise known as the Polar Bear . . ."

"We used to call that the Submarine, and when you put two shots of vodka in a glass and filled it up with sparkling wine it was a V2 Rocket, the same thing with three vodkas was a Soyuz 3, but I never had the courage to go for one of those. We also drank Pond Scum, Wolf Breath, that was hard to survive, we drank Chumbawamba, Korea, Bamboo Shoot with a Motor . . ."

"Bamboo Shoot with a Motor?"

"Red wine and cola, half-half, with a large shot of Fernet, it's an atrocious drink. We also drank Polish Flag, otherwise known as a Flamingo, but the worst drink of all was Traffic Light . . . We ordered a Traffic Light not so long ago with a certain Sasha Pernica in a restaurant in the Jizerské Mountains for old times' sake, and up there they also had no idea what we wanted. So we told them: Pour some cherry liqueur into a glass, then slowly pour in some advocaat and then some green mint liqueur, and there you have it. They were a little concerned, but they made it for us, though they improved it at the end, after all we're now living in a market economy, by chucking in some ice and giving it a stir . . . But seeing as you know all these cocktails, why are you so outraged by someone drinking a Magic Eye?"

"Because I'm not familiar with it and unfamiliar phenomena always lead to outrage. Well, there you go, I tried to bring you up as a decent person and this is the result . . ."

"There are worse cases. And anyway, your methods of upbringing were sometimes a little suspect, like that time you left me on my own in the forest."

"Which forest?"

"In Vídrholec, I couldn't have been older than four. We were out on a walk and as part of the adventure we climbed up into a hunting hide. We were sitting up there and you said you were just going to take a leak and come back and then you disappeared. You don't remember that?"

"Vídrholec is that part of the country when you go from Smolík in the direction of Ouvaly . . ."

"Of course it is!"

"Vídrholec . . . A long time ago it used to be a heavy insult when someone said: *You used to stand on Vídrholec!* The only way to counter that was by drawing blood, because you'd been accused of robbing and murdering wayfarers . . . Oh well, are you sure you didn't make this up?"

"I'm certain. I still see it like it happened yesterday, me sitting up there on this plank, my heart pounding, the silence, and the flies buzzing and dragonflies rattling . . . I waited for you for at least half an hour and then I climbed down from that damn high hide. You were still nowhere around, so I set out in the approximate direction of home, and only after a long time did I notice you watching me from a distance. At first I didn't know it was you and then I recognised you and instead of no longer being frightened I became really terrified because it seemed very strange for you to be hiding from me . . ."

"Maybe I wanted to see how you'd cope in an unusual situation, after all, what's intelligence? The ability to adapt to unfamiliar circumstances . . ."

"Well thanks very much for that. I almost shat myself from fear because before you disappeared you'd been telling me about ghouls and Kurupira."

"About what?"

"About Kurupira."

"I've no idea what you're talking about."

"Doesn't matter."

"Oh come on, explain, everything on earth has an explanation . . ."

"Well Kurupira is a monster that has blue teeth and lives in the jungle. You're the one who told me about it . . ."

"*Blue teeth?* Horseleg was a monster, my mother used to scare me with it, and also Scratchleg . . . Maybe I did abandon you in the forest, but you have to admit that otherwise I looked after you all my life, and you grew up to be at least a slightly normal person . . . But you hold on to that Hanka, she must be one of those rare kind-hearted girls if she can manage to stand you for more than a little while, how long have you been together?"

"Two and a half years."

"And listen, hope you're not being unfaithful to her!"

Goddamn it, what business is that of yours . . . the demon in my head roared, rattling my spinal cord and kicking the walls of my cranium: None of your fucking business . . . !

"No I'm not," I heard a forty-two-year-old son answer his seventy-one-year-old father. "Hanka is the first one I'm not being unfaithful to."

"Well I'm glad to hear that, it's none of my business, but you know that . . . I'd also like you to be doing well."

"I know, I'm doing OK."

"I hope so. You know, it's hard with you, you've never really loved anyone."

What's he talking about . . . , choked the little demon: Of course you have . . . ! For fuck's sake, haven't you gone through your fair share of torment . . . ! Pain and anguish?! Your fair share of suffering, you cripple . . . ?! Doesn't even your own father see that . . . ?!

"No, I haven't," I said, "I guess no one taught me how . . . Have you ever really loved anyone?"

"Unlike you I at least tried. I tried to love every woman I lived with, though it wasn't easy because I've never been with a woman who didn't want to take a bite out of a piece of bread I'd just buttered, didn't want to know what I was laughing about the moment I laughed or read at least a little bit out of the book I'd just opened . . . I tried to love Ivana. I tried to love you. And unlike you I never abandoned anyone . . ."

"Ahem."

"You see, that's all you've got to say."

"It would be a long conversation."

"One you don't want to start, that's the main thing."

"No I don't . . . But tell me, what happened in Yugoslavia during the war that was so bad people here wouldn't believe it, like you were saying back up on the hill?"

"Well, nothing pleasant . . . Take Ante Pavelić, the head of the Ustashi, there's proof that his faithful followers gave him eight kilos of eyeballs pickled in brine for his birthday . . . The thing was that Pavelić recruited his people in the same areas that Baron Trenck had done two hundred years before, in Slavonia, Hercegovina, and he probably knew exactly why. That region is full of *koljač*, how do you say that in Czech . . ."

"Cutthroats."

"Yep. That's the legacy of the Turks."

"Oh."

"Well, there were excesses, but it wasn't just about the leaders. For example, there was an incident when a teacher during a normal lesson in school told all the Serbian pupils to stand up, lined them up against the blackboard, and then cut their throats one by one in front of the other kids with his own knife . . . And there were many such cases, let's have another juniper brandy instead . . ."

"Over here! Another shot of the hard stuff!" a tousled youth in the corner under the coatrack called, waving his arms so that the waiter would notice him.

"Of course, not nearly everyone was a fanatic," Father continued.

"My father had a principle that a boss and his employees should be like a big family, and he was friends with most of his. For that reason the family of a woman called Števa used to come visit us, for many years she was his most faithful employee, and her brother, a barber, used to come with her and my father always drank rakija with him and they'd rant about politics, especially the Ustashi, you know. But then one day the barber arrived dressed in a Ustashi uniform, made a gesture with his hands and said: 'Well, it's come to this! I've joined them and that's that . . . ,' and at that moment you could literally see how it had rattled my father. But in the end things stayed the way they'd been, the barber kept coming round to our place, though he was shaving the chin and cutting the hair of Pavelić himself. I remember how he and my father used to laugh about it, drinking rakija, and my father was shouting in Croatian: *'Rudo, evo ti dvjesto hiljada, ako zakolješ Pavelića!'*, that he would give him two hundred thousand if he cut Pavelić's throat while shaving him, and the barber laughed: 'You'd better increase the sum, because if I went and reported what you asked me to do, they'd kill you without a thought and I'd get a medal for vigilance!' and they both laughed even more and my father opened another bottle and shouted: *'Rudo, dat ču ti tristo hiljada!'*, that he'd give three hundred thousand and the barber laughed, shouting: 'That's too little, raise the fee!' And my mother was crying in the kitchen because she knew that if nothing worse happened my father was going to be sick all the next day . . . You're laughing but it wasn't all that funny at the time, just one little thing was enough, you know," Father got up and disappeared in the smoke in the direction of the toilets.

After a while he reappeared and as he was nearing the table, he was saying: "Or there was this German guy by the name of Hügel who lived across the street from us a few years before the war, he was a famous football player and had a very beautiful wife, also German, and he was a big friend of my father's, they were always going fishing and on hiking trips. And then out of the blue Hügel joined the SS . . . I remember how one time he came over for dinner with his wife, by that time he was wearing his SS uniform and boots, they sat down, eating, conversing, and then I guess they had a few glasses and suddenly he jumped up and started shouting at my father: 'You bastard of a factory owner, we're going to come down hard on the likes of you soon enough, you'll see!' And his wife, this beauty, went pale, stood up and took her Hügel's service revolver out of its case on his belt and in front of everyone she put it to his head like this and said: 'You've got no right threatening these people! Apologise right now or I'll put a hole in your head right here! Well, what's it going to be? Apologise!' "

"Really?"

"Yep . . . and, believe it or not, he actually knocked his heels together, bowed, apologised, kissed my mother's hand, and off they went. But for a long time my father felt bad about it because the two of them used to be really good friends . . . Hügel then went off somewhere to the Eastern Front and just before the war he returned to Zagreb, where they immediately arrested him. They were going to execute him straightaway, him being an SS man, but my father backed him up, said he knew him and that he'd always been a decent fellow, so they only imprisoned him and my father would go to see him in the prison camp, he'd take him sardines and salami to make it more bearable. What they had going together, that was peculiar . . . With my own eyes I saw how that SS officer kneeled before him and cried: 'Zdenko, my friend,

I was such a terrible bastard and you've been so kind to me . . .
I won't forget this as long as I live!' "

Father talked and I listened. I took three matches out of the
box lying on the table, put their heads together, lit them with a
fourth match, blew the flame out, and stood them on the table.
Then I made a second tripod. Then a third.

"You've always been restless, no doubt about it," Father shook
his head.

"And you're the picture of serenity, I suppose?"

"I am now, at least to some extent, anyway, after those three
operations, but I've always been a little more steadfast than you,
at least I finished my studies and got a job I enjoyed, whereas
you live entirely from day to day . . ."

"Planning the future is like going fishing in a dry valley, nothing's ever like you intended it."

"Says who?"

"One guy."

"I know, you always find an excuse. I admit I'm not exactly the
right person to give you advice, but try for once to learn a lesson
from mistakes made by others!"

"A person only realises that something's a mistake once
they've made it themselves," my lips articulated, while a dry voice
rattled in my head: Whatever you do, don't act the tough guy
. . . ! Sit, drink, and don't act the tough guy . . . !

"Oh well, yeah, I guess that's true," Father took a swig of his
beer. "The fact is that I also always behaved as though someone
was looking over my shoulder . . . Like a third person giving the
second a very simplified report about what the first one thinks. I
behaved like I was writing some stupid soap opera about myself
so that it could even be understood even in an old peoples' home.

And I suspect this was how I managed to fuck up my entire life, more or less . . ."

"Is there any way not to fuck it up?" I said.

"Of course there *isn't*, but you at least have to try. I've started to realise of late that the samurai knew what they were doing, you see, a samurai warrior, when there's no way out of a predicament, sits down, stops paying attention to his surroundings, and goes on a journey *into his inner self.*"

"I'm familiar with that."

"You can't be," Father said with a little smirk, "you're only a tad over forty. When I was your age I had the world at my feet, I had the best time of my life between forty and fifty, there were so many women after me, I didn't even have time to process them all. Oh dear . . . If it was possible to turn the clock back, I'd certainly have no desire to be twenty again! If I could, I'd go back to being forty again, that was a much better age! By then, one's finally gotten rid of the worst foolishness but still has enough strength to really do something for a few years . . ."

"Hmm."

"For that matter, I remember when you were young you used to be quite dashing and not even that did you any good, judging by the women you lived with."

"Because I was totally confused. Now I've got a face like a monkey's arse and bags under my eyes, but inside I'm calm, sometimes even happy . . ."

"Happy? And what about . . . or for what reason?"

"That's the point, absolutely no reason, like you say, simply because I'm not twenty or thirty anymore and I don't have to decipher the incomprehensible mess of relationships over and over again . . ."

"Yeah, yeah, but *happy*, I can't ever remember being that . . . Are you happy *now* for example?"

"Not exactly right now when we're talking like this."

"Well there you go . . ."

"That was a joke."

"I get it."

"So why aren't you laughing?"

"Oh, because that humour of yours . . . Okay, at least you've got some sense of humour . . ."

"That's also why we can't really understand each other."

"But what are you talking about for goodness' sake, all my life people used to come to see me, in the factory, the laboratory, then at the institute, telling me: *Ivan*, we'd love to have that sense of *humour* of yours, nothing bothers you, you just always laugh at everything . . . Well, they were wrong there but that doesn't matter, the way I see it today, the best thing would've been not to think about anything at all and just live normally."

"I have to admit, I can't do that."

"Few people can. Of all the people I knew, the one who could do it best was Arno."

"Which Arno?"

"Arno Karin, my cousin, little Arnie, as my mother used to call him, he was an astonishingly merry person! He was born in Schönwald back in the days when that part of the country was still the Sudetenland, you know, his mother was my father's sister, she married a dentist who came from Schönwald . . ."

"And how did you know him if he was born in the Sudetenland and you were born in Zagreb?"

"They came to stay with us a few times during the summer for holidays. That dentist didn't talk at all, at least I don't recall hearing a single word from him, but Arno's mother laughed constantly, Arno took more after her . . . Well, and when the shit hit the fan in Bohemia in 1938, Arno packed up and ran away to Denmark. There he joined the British Army, went to England to be trained and then went to fight on the Italian Front. And there he also fought at the battle of Monte Cassino where he was lucky enough to get his nose shot off."

"That's a pretty strange bit of luck."

"It was lucky for Arno because when he was younger he had problems attracting women, he had a typical Jewish nose, like a gherkin, in general he looked like a genuine son of Moses . . . And when they shot that nose off he was taken to a military hospital and a plastic surgeon there made him a gorgeous little new nose, one of those Anglo-Saxon snub noses. And dear Arno became more confident, grew himself a thin moustache like an American actor, and became a bit of a fop. Meanwhile the war ended and by the time we met here in Bohemia he already had both his hands full of women, walking around Prague in his English uniform with that little nose of his, putting all his efforts into catching up on what he'd neglected, ladies, young girls, like I said."

"And what happened to his parents in Schönwald?"

"What do you think happened, they went up in smoke . . . Arno went to look for them as soon as he got here but there were strangers living in their house who didn't know, or didn't want to say, what had happened to them, I don't think he ever even found out where they ended up, but how could he have suspected, you know . . . Then when we lived with Arno at our aunt's place in Ouvaly, I remember him singing all day, he loved operettas, he kept whistling: *When I see your eyes, I don't realise why I love my solitude so much, my dear girl*, but when he shaved in the mornings, he'd always stare at himself for a very long time, then he'd go to the garden and sit there smoking, looking up at the sky, but after breakfast he was all fun and laughter again. Auntie never left anyone alone for long, Ouvaly was a merry place, I remember how Auntie smashed an umbrella into pieces over my other cousin's back . . ."

"What for?"

"Oh it was something insignificant. The beating took place in the hallway, you see it was narrow and there was nowhere to dodge, and Auntie kept whacking her until it disintegrated, she was a great tennis player with a renowned forehand . . ."

"What about Arno, is he still alive?"

"Arno? He packed up his stuff after 1948 and went to Israel where he joined the army again right away. That's also where he died in battle, during the first Suez Crisis. Apparently they shot him as he was checking out some suspicious vehicle."

"Ah."

"But you know, it was hard to put up with all those women in Ouvaly anyway, there was always a scandal of some kind. The only exception was your cousin Soňa, I don't think she ever had a man her entire life, she was more interested in animals . . ."

"What?"

"Well she always had at least six cats, four dogs, a rook, lizards, newts, she had terrapins, of course, guinea pigs, stick insects, a slowworm, a swan, recently she picked up a toad somewhere, and as far as I remember she also had an owl but it died, no man could really stand it for long in Ouvaly, Uncle preferred to die in the end and Franta, he died in a car accident, you know. There's a guy called Miloš there now, but he won't last long either . . ."

"What owl?"

"Owl? I said Miloš."

"I know, but you said there used to be an owl and it died."

"Oh that, it was a *Bubo bubo*, an Eagle Owl, it was injured in some way and Soňa brought it home and nursed it back to health, at one time she even got the notion to get a bear but luckily Auntie never got to hear about it . . . But otherwise Auntie was really good friends with my mother, when those two got together my father had to either leave or have a Limping Pilgrim to get his courage up . . ."

"Limping Pilgrim?"

"Yep, that's what he called Georgian cognac. One time Auntie came to visit us at Klánovice, you hadn't been born yet, my parents were inside and I was reading out in the garden. And my father suddenly ran out the door and round the house several times, he was so upset, and every time he ran past me he shouted: Ivan, never get married! Mark my words! Never get married!"

"Yeah well . . . ," I said.

"Yeah well, yeah . . . ," Father said.

"Another shot of the hard stuff!" the young guy in the corner shouted, gesticulating like he was trying to climb a ladder.

I took three more matches out of the box and made another tripod. This time it fell apart as soon as I set it on the table.

"Well, to your health," Father said.

"To your health," I said and felt the froth running out of the corners of my mouth to my chin and from my chin down my shirt.

THE HOUSE

Later as I stood above the slime-coated urinal, slowly draining my bladder, the house that Father used to run around, the house I've been trying to forget about for thirty-five years, appeared before my eyes again. Once more I saw the ivy-covered villa at the edge of the wood, surrounded by Thujas, the nest I was hatched in, mummified with mothballs. I saw the terraces again. The sun-baked shutters. The hallways. That huge room on the ground floor whose dimensions were big enough to act as a substitute for the world outside. The room and the kitchen with the fridge that quivered rudely and the etched-glass panelling. The panelling covered by flocks of haplessly parading pink flamingos and pelicans that Father had painted there one day with acetone paints under the pretext that it would improve the appetite of his little son who sat under them every day poking about in his plate of mashed food. I saw the stairway that inevitably formed the backbone of the house, those creaking stairs covered by a worn carpet, held in place by hollow brass tubes that made gargling noises. I closed my eyes and walked up the stairs to the floor above. In front of me swayed a hall with many doors. Behind one vibrated a high-ceilinged and cold bathroom, closets and little bedrooms pulsated behind the others. And then there was one more door, the most interesting, because behind it was a forgotten chamber, a long and narrow room extending round a corner with a wooden ceiling petering out somewhere high up in the gloom. This door was always locked, but this did not prevent me from spending time there as often as I could. The way I normally accomplished this was by walking out of the house, stamping and coughing, walking back and forth in the garden for a while, and then returning as quietly as possible via the back door, taking the key from the peg and stealthily making my way upstairs, treading on the outside edge of the stairs where there was less risk of making them creak. I would unlock the door carefully and then lock it behind me again. And then I'd be inside. A different, considerably more attractive world awaited there, a world inhabited by armchairs torn at the seams, tabourets perforated by woodworm, wardrobes lamenting audibly, and long rows of shelves extending up to the ceiling, shelves filled with old clogs, cracked glass vases, copper cezves, and wax-spattered candleholders. Flints. Riding boots. Bayonets. Pikes. Bootjacks. Tin toys marbled with rust. Fractured steam trains that ran on solid fuel. Porcelain statuettes. Frowning plaster busts. Beaten-metal Balkan yatagans. Walking sticks. Boxes. Chests. Containers. Trinkets. Crates full of mouldy postcards and crooked nails. Animal skulls that would emerge from the depths of dark corners. Terrifyingly content, smiling Buddha statues. Goggle-eyed dragons curling like worms round fat enamelled Chinese vases in the shape of goose bellies. Memorial wreaths. Snuffers. Pliers. Strange pointed hammers with decorative handles. Trumpets. Hats. Faded snakes preserved in spirit. Tortoise shells. Empty-eyed papier-mâché masks, liable to change their expression depending on whether one was just frightened or breathless with terror. Huge iron alarm clocks crowned with battered bells. Bottles containing red, yellow, green, and black liquids. Thinners. Wires. Spools of shoemaker's hemp thread. Chains. Tins. Bouquets of caked paintbrushes. Wooden caskets panelled with mother-of-pearl, concealing rusty razors, shaving brushes, and blackened rings. I would leaf through bound volumes of the children's magazine *Punťa*. Full of sweet trepidation I delved into prewar story books with illustrations reminiscent of tableaux from hell. I stared at bald monkeys that looked like old men, at ferocious babbling monkeys counting coconuts, which upon closer inspection became dried human skulls. I ogled at the decaying, wrinkled faces of hedgehogs and dogs and mice. When a real witch peeped at me from between the pages it brought great relief from those thin-legged, sparsely-haired creatures that rather unpleasantly reminded me of eighty-year-old pensioners from Klánovice. The house resonated with bangs as Mother tenderised pork schnitzels downstairs. A jay screeched behind the window. Snails crunched their way through pine needles. The sound of a diesel engine grunting, rails rattling, and wires ringing drew closer through the woods. I unwrapped framed paintings covered with newspapers blackened by dust. On one painting, a woman's figure shroud in garments from head to toe walked up a steep, sun-drenched street at the end of which a thin high minaret protruded above the roofs. The woman ascended, slapping the pounded earth with her bare feet, the sky maddeningly blue, and — from my observing it for hours on end — the minaret gently, but clearly, swayed from side to side.

I shook my dick and put it back in my trousers. I spat into the urinal. I rinsed my hands. I knew exactly what would always bother me: Not the fact that they sold it all dirt cheap to some dealer after Granddad died, fuck the money. But that the house was the only and last place in my life where I was able to feel real mystery.

Go on, feel sorry for yourself . . . , the little demon chimed in. Feel sorry for yourself, you cripple . . . ! Sorry . . . ! Look forward for once, not backwards . . . ! Look ahead . . . !

"But nothing's there," I said quietly.

Nor *anywhere else* . . . , the demon screamed: Not behind you either . . . ! Ha, ha . . . ! Ha, ha! Hahahahahaha . . . !

I opened the door of the loo.

"A shot of the hard stuff!" reached my ears. "Over here . . . ! Bring me a stiff one!"

Father was tilting his beer mug and watching the arrows, crystal shapes, arcs, and curves flitting about on the tablecloth.

"Fancy this," I said as I sat down, "apparently during the time of the recent war in Bosnia all the woods around Ljubljana were full of bears. It seems there were so many of them that the bears themselves became nervous being together in one place like that, let alone the people, who were terrified to even go there . . ."

"And how did those poor beasts get there? There wasn't any fighting in those parts, was there?"

"They were bears from Bosnia and Croatia that had been driven out by the shooting and the shelling. They simply moved in the only direction that no gunfire was coming from, up into Slovenia."

"And where do you know this from?"

"From a Slovenian from Ljubljana."

"And where did you run across a Slovenian?"

"He was dating one of my friends."

"And what does he do?"

"All I know is he paints stage sets in a theatre in Ljubljana, maybe he's also a graphic artist or something . . . By the way, who painted those flamingos on the glass in the kitchen in the house in Klánovice? You?"

"Me, who else . . . I painted those for your benefit, it was your grandma's idea, so that you wouldn't mind spending time in the kitchen and would eat better, you might have been three years old, or so. Originally, I wanted to paint a tiger shark munching a diver, but everyone was in agreement, which was a rare thing indeed, that it wasn't a good idea because they said you would be *frightened* by it. So I started painting a sperm whale struggling with a giant squid, but they claimed *they* wouldn't like that, so I didn't bother arguing and made those dumb flamingos . . . What made you remember that just now?"

"Don't know, really."

"I knew a woman in Ljubljana, she was a real woman that one, thin, but what a figure, just a glance at her was enough to give me a belly-slapping erection, even though she had these really tiny breasts, as soon as I touched them I could tell they'd gone hard, I know father and son shouldn't be talking to each other like this, but who's left in the world for me to tell it to, you know . . . And she had these freckles down on her back which looked exactly like the five on dice. Her brother was a former army officer and he taught me to trim a hedge with a cutlass and while I was doing it I almost sliced their old aunt in half, she was walking along the path with the shopping. I got such a fright they had to give me a shot of liquor to revive me, and as for the aunt? She laughed for another two days . . ."

"About fifteen years ago I was going out with, or seeing, once in a while, this woman . . ."

"I get it. And?"

"Well, nothing, she was just my type, not too big, her legs weren't too long, basically thin, but not as thin as a tailor's dummy . . ."

"Tailor's dummies don't tend to be very thin."

"Exactly! And this girl also had black eyebrows, black eyes, and blond hair, and her face looked like a warm wind had been blowing on it her entire life. Back then she already had two kids . . . So anyway, recently, about a year and a half ago, I walked into a club I got invited to and who did I see? This Pavlína was standing by the bar, looking at me. My heart almost jumped into my throat because she hadn't changed at all in those fifteen years, the same hair, figure, wire-frame glasses on her nose, the same expression, still with that look on her face like she was on a roller coaster! So I walked up to her and said: 'Hello!' And she laughed, tapped her cigarette and said: 'Oh yeah, yeah, I remember you, hang on, you're that Honza Beneš!' And I started telling her stories and I couldn't keep my eyes off her and as I was talking away, saying whatever came into my head, I asked her: 'And where do you live right now, Pavlína?' and Pavlína pushed her glasses back and said: 'But I'm Ája, ha ha, that's funny, you thought I was my mum!' and she pointed behind her, and over in the corner a wrinkly old blonde grandmother sat drinking wine, and this crooked granny looked up, adjusted her glasses and said: 'Greetings, you still alive?' So I went over to where she sat and we talked and I kept eyeing her daughter, whom I remembered as a five-year-old, Pavlína kept nodding, drinking sour Frankovka wine, and then she suddenly yelled at her daughters, they were both there, and they both looked like her on a photograph from fifteen years ago: 'OK girls, time to go, hop it, got a tram to catch, we're paying up and getting out of here!' "

"Oh well, the worst, and maybe the best, thing about women is that they're jealous about everything, they even take a solar eclipse or a rainstorm personally. But never mind that, I wanted to ask you something . . . Why exactly are you here, do you even know?"

"Because you made me."

"Well that's true, sorry about that, it happens . . . But why do you live in *Prague* all your life?"

"Because I'm afraid of changing my life for the worse. Prague is the only place where I can live."

"And how do you know that if you've never tried it anywhere else?"

"Spending a week or two in some other town is more than enough time for me to see that I'd go bonkers from the nothingness, the lack of ambiguity, the *seriousness* of people's lives there. Once you become a *tailor* there, all you can do is tow the line and remain a *tailor* until you die because that's how everyone sees you no matter how hard you try to be something else."

"And what don't you like about that?"

"It's boring! To take on one role and act it out until you completely decompose!"

"Whereas here?"

"Life unfolds here as if it were a comedy by Frič, or some touchingly naff Italian porno . . . Like the assassination of Heydrich performed by a children's puppet theatre . . ."

"And you like that?"

"I like that very much."

"What, for goodness' sake, do you like about it?"

"The theatrical dimensions, the small space. The way a gangster has a similar social standing to a minister, and vice versa. All the clowning. All the messing around and rubbing of elbows . . . All those stories about how someone used to drink beer and play cards with the president . . ."

"A total circus."

"But a merry one."

"Well, if it were me I'd go off somewhere at once! A long time ago a technical book of mine was published in Brazil and I was supposed to go there as a result, but because my Uncle Pavel still lived in São Paulo at the time, I somehow knew that if they let me go I wouldn't come back. But you and Ivana were too little for me to leave you, so I decided to forget about it and didn't go. My ideal was to live the last part of my life somewhere abroad where no one would know and need me. To disappear somewhere by the sea or in the jungle . . . To get lost in a wet green rainforest and never come back, never and to no one, oh well."

"Pavel was the one who spent the entire war at the embassy in Budapest, wasn't he?"

"At the Portuguese Embassy in Budapest, how come today of all days you keep asking about people you've never had any interest in?"

"I'm getting old."

"You're getting old but you're not old, there's a huge difference . . . Originally, Uncle Pavel didn't speak a word of Portuguese, you know, he only knew Czech and Hungarian, but during those five years, when he could never even go out on the street, he became so familiar with Portuguese that after the war he moved straight to Lisbon and from Lisbon he went to be a bank clerk in São Paulo where he got married to a black woman twenty-five years his younger. Oh yes, Brazil . . . But you've been to Lisbon, haven't you?"

"I have. Had swordfish there."

"And how do you know it was swordfish?"

"It was written on the menu. I know, they can write what they feel like."

"That's right!"

"But what I wanted to say was that I've got this girlfriend who went to Peru this year . . ."

"A moment ago you said you were being faithful to Hanka."

"This one's just a friend."

"And what was she doing in Peru, poor thing?"

"She wanted to see what it's like there. She stayed in some village with a Czech painter. And when she came back she said how in this remote village on the edge of the jungle there lives a little boy that goes by the name of Hitler."

"Is that his surname?"

"That's the point, it's his first name. You see, his parents heard that there used to be someone famous with that name but they didn't know exactly who, so they gave him the first name Hitler. 'Hitlercito!' they call to him in the village, 'Hitlercito, go get us some cigs!' and off he goes and brings them because he's a really kind and obliging and handsome boy and everyone there likes him."

"I'd be off somewhere at the drop of a hat, even to Peru, even if every other person there was called Hitler," Father sighed, "but nowadays I can hardly walk, what would they do with me there . . . Back when I could have gone you were still kids and now I'm an old man . . ."

"Well, don't complain all the time, for God's sake," I said.

"I'm not complaining, I told you I don't know how it's done."

"You've been complaining as long as I've known you. Just take things as they are!"

"Yeah, yeah, you don't know what it's like yet when people you know are getting old and going senile and keep repeating themselves and die, the women want something from you all the time, but don't say exactly what, and when you give it to them they leave you. And the kids laugh at you because they think their life is going to be different, better somehow."

"I know a bit about it. I've got a few friends who aren't even forty yet and already they keep saying the same things over and over, and I smile at them and pretend that everything's fine because the only other option is to get used to being alone. Come to think of it, recently I've noticed that people get fidgety when I'm talking about something and when I ask what's wrong they say: 'Nothing, all good, it's just that you already told me that the day before yesterday . . .' "

"Oh, but look here, you're having fun in this world! You like it here! My father also liked life till the day he died because he was a tyrannical and irate sort of man and because he was always getting angry at everything, he never had any time for ideals such as achieving a state of *non-existence* and that sort of thing . . . And you take after him entirely, after all he always saw himself in you! One time he had a huge crate with a construction kit delivered for you all the way from Italy . . ."

"I know, it was a Merkur Constructo."

"That's right, Merkur. My father upheld that sort of kitschy old patriarchal principle that only the best is good enough. Though when I was a kid and asked for a toy, hell I got an earful, all I had was a tin sailor that was permanently saluting, I wanted a proper rifle but my father said no, so I made one out of wood and whenever I pointed it at an adult I made a loud farting noise. Then someone told my parents on me and I got such a smack at lunchtime my forehead hit the table, the thing was, though, there was a bowl of soup right in front of me and the soup spilled into the lap of a certain Aunt Olja who was visiting us, I think my father secretly fancied her, so I got another one good and proper

. . . Well, come to think of it, I didn't have any toys even though my father had a toy factory! That was unfortunately his view on how to raise kids . . ."

"I had enough toys."

"Yes you did, you came along later."

"I had that Dakota on floats, then I had that rocket, which flew fairly high if you pumped it up to the limit . . ."

"I'm well aware of that, you broke a window with it and I had to replace the glass."

"Sorry about that. I also had a pneumatically-powered Bakelite submarine . . ."

"I remember that one . . ."

"I liked it a lot but it sank in that muddy pond by the train tracks . . ."

"You had me go fetch it and I sliced my leg open trying, so there it stayed . . ."

"A battery-powered bulldozer, a tractor of some kind, a metal steamroller, two tanks that made sparks, an ordinary one and one that was optimistically modified for use on Mars, a diver, or *nurek*, he had a flat face printed in colour stuck to the glass on the inside of his helmet and it looked exactly like the face of Ferenc Futurist . . . Then I had that plastic construction set which consisted of little coloured parts with holes and bolts, yellow and red and black and orange and green banana-shaped bits that looked edible and in fact one time I couldn't help myself and swallowed a few of the little bananas. Then for a week afterwards I poked about in my shit to see if they'd come out yet."

"And did they?"

"They never did. Maybe they're still in me somewhere."

"I remember that before the war my father's biggest contracts weren't for toys, orders mostly came for mannequins for clothes shops . . . One time he got a big order from a department store in Sarajevo and they wanted a lot of male mannequins, so my father sent a wagon load of them, but after a while they all came back. So off he went to Sarajevo to ask in person what they didn't like about his shop dummies. And the boss of the store invited him in and started shouting: 'What you sent me weren't male mannequins at all, you must be pulling my leg, I'm not going to pay for that!' 'What's the matter with them?' my father asked. 'You've still got the nerve to ask what's wrong with them?' the director screamed, 'they don't have the main thing that makes a man a man!' 'And what would that be?' my father asked, somewhat dumfounded by this time. And the director almost collapsed: 'How can you even ask that! Can't you see!? *It doesn't have a moustache!!!*' So my father went back and had a proper moustache added to each mannequin, put them on the train again, and only then was Sarajevo happy."

"He was always scheming," I said, "two or three years before his death he was telling me how he'd invented some kind of patented beehive and that he was getting ready to convert the garage to make the beehives to order . . ."

"When was that?"

"Like I said, a few years before he died. I was in Klánovice for summer holidays at the time."

"Oh, that's right, you did go there for the holidays."

"Of course I did . . . When the Russians stormed in I spent two entire months there. That was a strange holiday, someone always ringing the doorbell, people with faces drained of colour sitting in the armchair all the time, blowing into their handkerchiefs, drinking coffee, and saying: 'What a situation, you've been abroad, Mr. Beneš, what do you think about all this?' And Grandfather just waved his arm, poured them a cognac, and said: 'They've swallowed us up, Mr. Skružný, oh well! What's there to tell, Mr. Březina, alas!' I can still see it like it was yesterday, how one morning he grabbed my hand and said 'Come on!' and we went to the road that goes from Újezd by the viaduct, along which tanks had been rolling from morning till night for about four days."

"Oh . . . and what did you do there?"

"We stood on the pavement, Granddad held my hand and at regular intervals repeated: *See that? Remember it! See that? Remember it!*"

"Well, you see, you remember it . . ."

"I remember it like it happened the day before yesterday because it was the first time I'd seen real tanks. What a rush! The motors roared, smoke hung above the woods, the tanks rumbled along one after another, and still there was no end to them! And we stood there until the afternoon. Granddad shook his fist at them but I waved at them, secretly so he couldn't see it . . . I remember one tiny officer with a moustache and one of those broad flat caps of theirs who kept looking round at us from an armoured car and he just couldn't get it: grandfather threatening, little boy waving . . ."

"But you were ten by then, you might have understood what was going on."

"But that's the thing, I did! The way everyone was trying to play both sides, hedge their bets one way or the other, full of talk about socialism with a human face but scared shitless at the same time, my family too, Mother and Pepík, all the time fooling around with *pamphlets* of some sort but making sure the neighbours didn't notice. I felt nauseated by it all. I was glad Granddad was shaking his fist, at least that was something, but at the same time I really liked those tanks, so naturally I preferred to wave . . . In the end Granddad picked up a small stone from the pavement and sort of demonstratively, so that everyone would see, threw it at one of the tanks."

"That's just like him, he had a sense for showmanship in every situation, or how to put it . . . It helped him survive, that's for sure. When they let him out of prison, he went to work as a manual labourer in the ČKD machine factory, made his way up to skilled labourer, then foreman, and in the end they wanted him to be technical manager but he preferred to retire . . . Did he hit it?"

"Hit what?"

"The tank."

"He did."

"Oh well," Father said pensively. "My father and I never really did see eye to eye. From an early age his principle that money can do anything really pissed me off . . . Once, a long time ago when I was a child, I won a swimming race and brought home a medal, and instead of congratulating me he says: 'Ivan, I hope, however, that you don't think you can swim better than your mother!' and I just laughed and he started screaming: 'You can't swim better than your mother because she was taught by a *professional swimming coach!*' by which he meant *with his money*, you know, it was one of those coaches that had my mother on a sort of fishhook when she was in the water, shouting out: 'One two three, one two three . . .' But my father was firmly convinced that this is the only way someone can learn to swim. That it's not possible for someone to learn to swim properly *for free*. There's no two ways about it, he was a real capitalist. And as a result I had this ideal that one day, when I finally became independent, money would not be important to me. That if I ever had any I'd go out and spend it without any fuss," Father said, and his eye twitched. He looked as though he'd just realised something.

I couldn't help recalling his tiny first-floor bedsit in Prague-Spořilov. The rotten wardrobe, the mouldy bathroom, the cheap mass-produced furniture, the rows of dusty bottles amongst piles of grime beneath the kitchen sink.

I said nothing.

Father said nothing.

The demon said nothing, biting his claws.

"Which I guess I probably managed in the end . . ." Father said after a good five minutes.

"Two more beers?" the sweat-drenched publican said, leaning over us.

"Yep," Father said.

"No, that'll be all, we'll have the bill," I said.

"Well, what's it going to be?" the publican asked.

"Two junipers and we'll pay up," I said.

"That'll be two junipers," the publican sang to himself.

"Over here . . . ! A shot of the hard stuff!" the young fellow in the corner demanded, his throat dry.

"You're right, juniper brandy's a better choice," Father said. "And what about you, off in a hurry somewhere again?"

"Not really, I'm just a little tired."

"And what from, for goodness' sake."

"I don't get a breather all day!"

"Doing what?"

"Trying to meet the demands placed on an adult individual."

"But your biggest problem has always been that you simply

don't want to be an adult," said a seventy-one-year-old to a forty-two-year-old.

"That's the same thing you told me in a dream last night," I said.

"Well I'm not surprised you're tired when you dream about me . . . And what was I doing in the dream?"

"You were watching the sea."

"Oh yeah, that's what I'd like to be doing in reality as well, that could never become ordinary," Father said nodding.

"Over here! A stiff one!" the youth in the corner clamoured, waving his arms above his head, but no one took any notice.

I got up and walked off in the direction of the loo.

I hadn't had the dream the previous day. It had been roughly a month earlier. Humans can't help themselves: they always have to modify, simplify, fine-tune reality. Cultivate. Cut it up and splice it together again. The result tends to be a kind of bathhouse intimacy, the familiarity of stage sets, which becomes annoying after a while. But then again, what happens in the next ten minutes is always incomparably more important than what the world will be like in a year's time.

The dream was about my standing on a beach by the sea with Father. The beach was only a few metres wide, but it stretched along the whole coast, from one end of the horizon to the other. Directly behind it a pine forest rustled, and between the forest and the beach there were endless rows of abandoned corrugated-iron stalls. The sand beneath our feet was dark grey, fine, full of broken glass and branches and bottle tops and similar rubbish. Even the sea was grey, and the steep swelling waves drew lazily towards the shore. Somehow the water seemed to be thick like porridge. Suddenly, not far away from us, a bare grey-pink hump rolled over in the waves. Rolled over and vanished. Then it reappeared a little further away. Then it rolled over again and disappeared again. "Did you see that?" I said. "Sure," Father replied, "before the war there used to be lots of them around here, but now, it's entirely possible that's the last one . . ." "What

is it?" I asked. "Don't you recognise it? Watch it for a while, then
. . ." The humped back appeared again and disappeared again.
Then a huge, child-like face surfaced, looked at us and then
submerged. I caught a glimpse of the eyes in the great doughy
face, and they were full of inexpressible sadness. "Well, do you
know now?" Father asked. "I do," I exhaled, because after that I
preferred not to know. I was standing in the sand, watching the
low purple horizon with dull anxiety in my heart. Rather than
waiting for it to re-emerge, I decided to turn round, walk over to
the forest and have a look at it. I walked between the kiosks,
stopped by the first tree, and started to urinate. As I was finishing,
I noticed a little table by the tree. A small child was sitting
behind it and watching in mute amazement as my piss splashed
the pages of a picture book. I turned round quickly and returned
to the sea. Father was still standing on the same spot, watching
the rolling outlines of the waves. "Have you noticed that at this
moment memories are already forming, right here in the present,
right before our eyes?" he asked. "Sure, this is how I spend my
time from morning to night," I replied. "Oh, that's right, you
manufacture memories, I might have known . . ." he replied
morosely, "and how do you do this?" "I simply concentrate on the
mystery." "Oh, the mystery, well I'd rather not even know what
you mean by that . . . There are some casemates over there, or
something like that, let's go take a look," he said. And sure
enough, in the distance the beach was interrupted by a long
building running far out to sea. We headed towards it. We
walked and walked. Our feet got stuck in the dunes, the waves
rolled, the foam sparkled, and the wind blew. Still, it all seemed
to have been arranged in a shoe box, as though the windswept
horizons were about three to four metres away from us all the

time. In the end we shuffled over to a Renaissance palace covered in cracks, which was only remarkable for one reason: it stood right in the water. There was a large inscription carved in stone in a curve above the entrance: DAS RÄTSEL GIBT ES NICHT. "What is it with you and German, it's a terrible language," Father said reproachfully. "But I didn't write it there," I objected. "Can you at least tell me what it means?" "I don't know what *Rätsel* means," I shrugged my shoulders. "I don't either, let's go take a look, maybe we'll find out," Father said. We patted the sand off our feet and walked into a long, cold hallway decorated from floor to ceiling in tedious Mediterranean frescos, lots of dolphins and naked women and palm trees and archers and harpies. It started to dawn on me that we had entered someone's private space and had no business being there. After a while, the hollow clapping of heels reverberated in the distance. Two female figures in pale dresses were walking towards us along the balustrade. I quickly checked if we were dressed appropriately. I was wearing a shirt and sandals, but I had on neither trousers nor underwear. My dick was hanging from under my shirt. But before I had time to get concerned, Father waved his hand ostentatiously, sighed and said: "Oh yeah, I noticed . . . What should we do with you, eh! That's always been your problem, you simply refuse to act grown-up, no matter what . . . I wonder how you'll explain yourself now!"

I stared at the scratched wall in front of me covered with messages written in ballpoint pen. *You poor bastard, you're going to get your head kicked in! Shut the fuck up, you fucking shitface! I voted for the Communist Party! You belong on a reservation! White Power! Budmerice Barracks — 147 day to go! Praguers are fucking cunts!* I read.

Once again you've no idea which way the wind blows . . . ! the little demon raised his voice from the back of my mind.

"No one knows," I answered, somewhat taken aback that suddenly the intonation of my voice was identical to that of Father's, "everyone only suspects. Or they at least try to pretend."

There's nothing mysterious about the way the world *looks* . . . The mystery is that the world exists *at all!* the demon mumbled, chillingly: Do you know that . . . ?! Do you, or don't you . . . ?!

"Damn it, they're only stage sets," I said in Father's voice. "Compulsive, flat imaginings," I said in Father's voice. "The only reason why the world exists is that I want it to, because I'm afraid of what would be if it didn't," I added in Father's voice.

Surprisingly, the little demon shut up. Maybe he didn't expect that I could be such a nitwit. Maybe there is some world outside of me, the thought occurred to me. Maybe for real. Maybe it all really does *exist!*

Rat-tat . . . rat-tat . . . rat-tat rat-tat rat-tat . . . , the little demon stammered: Yes! Yes! Yes, yes, yes, yes, yes, yes, yes . . . !

I waved my arm and opened the door. Father was standing in a trance in the middle of the room, the light of a bulb shining through his sparse white hair, splashing on his worried head. He was watching a topless waitress caked in make-up taking mugs of Staropramen round the pub. I closed the door and walked up to him.

"Come on, Dad, don't stand about here . . . ," I said.

"Hold on, let me be, I know, you can see this whenever you feel like it, and maybe even when you don't, but I haven't seen a woman as young as this for years!" Father answered.

"Come and sit down, though, she's not going anywhere."

We sat back down. The baby doll took round pickled sausages and pickled hermelín cheese, as well as yellowy, approximately half-filled half-litres. Her eyebrows were shaved and instead she had two cruel curves pencilled on her forehead, making her look totally washable. This was another opportunity to observe that strange phenomenon when almost all the guys suddenly quiet down and their eyes get shifty. The way they start ordering coffee, trying to sound proper. The way the backs of the necks of the blond guys turn red. How they wink at each other, but only once the man-eater has walked off.

"Where did she spring from?" I asked.

"I'm not even sure, really, I went over there to get matches, you know, and she suddenly appeared and took me completely by surprise . . . I know it's the fashion now, but when I was young you had to go to a brothel to get something like that, though nowadays every place is a whorehouse . . . Oh well, you know I always wanted to do it with a Japanese woman . . . at least one time in my life . . . and she wouldn't even have to be all that pretty . . . but I never did get one . . ."

"I slept with a Chinese woman."

"Chinese, I don't envy you that at all," Father waved his arm, "Japanese, that's something entirely different, I wanted a Japanese . . . and I never did manage it . . ."

"I'd be afraid of a Japanese woman, they have that code of honor . . . ," I was saying, observing the way the pub had started to sway before my eyes again, swinging twice to the left, once to the right, and then left again. Chaos.

"What code?"

"A code of honor . . ."

"I'd have no fear of a Japanese woman," Father said, lowering his voice. "I admit that half my life I was afraid of whores, because I had no idea the only difference between them and other women is that they make things less complicated. If I'd known that earlier, I could have avoided quite a few predicaments . . ."

"I, on the contrary, have been afraid of kind women all my life," I said, "because I know sooner or later we'll have nothing to say to each other, because unfortunately only the bitches have that vibrant magic, good women almost never do."

"That's true, but sometimes you end up making a real blunder. One time I got duped in Karlovy Vary, this woman with a beautiful hairdo was sitting there, hair like Sofia Loren, and she was winking at me, making no secret of it, so okay, I ordered cognac and invited her for a drink. But right away she started confiding in me, saying she's a widow and she feels like crying because all men think about one thing only. Well, in the end she took me back to her place, being very coy about the whole thing, she wanted to talk about her varicose veins in the kitchen at three in the morning. So finally I managed to sweet-talk her into going to bed. Then she took her hair off, she had a wig on, you know, and then she took her sweater off, her ribs were like a rake, but I didn't mind because she had big solid tits, but then she took off those as well, she had mattress foam in her bra, you know, and to top it off she took out her teeth, so that we could kiss, she said, but by that time I was running like blazes, it was night and I had to sleep at the train station. You get all kinds of cases . . . I just want you to stay with Hanka, that's all. I hope you're not being unfaithful to her . . ."

"Why do you keep on about that today?"

"Well, it's because I see it all around me, Iva was with Fanda for many years, you know, and in the end he got up and without a word of explanation left her and she was left to deal with everything all by herself . . ."

"That can happen. I was rather fond of Fanda."

"And how's that possible, *you* hardly knew him?"

"Probably because of that idea of his about how to get in the Guiness Book of Records."

"I don't know about that . . ."

"He decided to walk from Prague to Vienna on stilts."

"Oh that, but that wasn't Fanda, that was some colleague of his from their painting and decorating firm . . ."

"But he told me it was his idea!"

"At least you see what he's like! He told me it occurred to a colleague of his, but I don't remember what happened exactly anymore . . ."

"Well, he'd fretted his whole life about not being anyone and not meaning anything and that no one knew about him and for once he'd like to accomplish something major . . . So he applied for a record attempt, got official registration, even got a sponsor it seems, and so finally he got up on the stilts. They made quite a show of it, had a picture taken and off he went. He only managed to walk two hundred metres and then got a hernia the size of a melon . . . They called an ambulance, he threw the stilts in a ditch, and that was the end of the record attempt," I said, laughing spasmodically.

Father's expression was neutral.

"And what was his reason for leaving Iva?" I changed tack back to the main theme.

"Why do men leave women, because of another woman, of course!"

"Aha," I said. "In fact, I remember now at one point I was almost sort of unfaithful to Hanka, but luckily it was with a woman whose name I didn't know, or even what she looked like."

"You'd better explain this one to me . . ."

"Well one day I was at home and I was supposed to go out somewhere, but I wasn't feeling too well, I was coming down with something, so I picked up the phone and wrote a text message: SORRY, GOT FLU, STAYING IN. And a few seconds later came a reply: GOOD IDEA, DONT GO ANYWHERE, FLU CAN BE SERIOUS, THOUGH HAVE NO IDEA WHO YOU ARE. K."

"K. who?"

"I was wondering that myself: WHAT DOES K. STAND 4? I asked. K. CAN STAND 4 LOTS OF THINGS, KRISTYNA, KLAUDIE, KLARA, KATERINA, KAREL & WHAT DOES 603275210 MEAN? came the reply. HONZA BENES WITH DIACRITICAL ABOVE S, I confessed straightaway, so there'd be no confusion. & WHERE R U? she wanted to know. IN BED, I punched. & WHAT CAN U SEE THRU YOUR WINDOW, U DO HAVE A WINDOW? she asked. OF OPPORTUNITY? I retorted. HA HA & WHAT CAN

YOU SEE THRU IT? she answered. ZIZKOV. LOOKS LIKE SOMEONE DREW IT THERE, I tapped. THRU MY WINDOW THERES SMICHOV, LOOKS LIKE SOMEONE DUMPED IT THERE. HAVE A NICE TIME & LIE DOWN! So I lay down and fell asleep. WHAT R THE BUGS UP 2? I read when I woke up. THEY R MULTIPLYING, I wrote and thought about how a virus actually multiplies when in fact it's simpler than a cell . . ."

"But it doesn't actually," Father grumbled. "A virus simply injects its DNA into the cell it is attacking, the cell disintegrates, becoming one or more new viruses. A virus is basically just DNA or RNA wrapped up in protein, a typical simple parasite, it doesn't even have any enzymes, a normal cell has several hundred of those . . . So what's the story with this woman then? I don't understand it at all."

"Well, like I was saying, I was lying in bed and we were texting each other, at first it was just a kind of conversation and after about a week it started getting quite personal."

"After a week?"

"We ended up writing to each other for three weeks."

"I'd go bonkers corresponding with a woman for three weeks."

"It was entertaining, she was funny."

"And what for goodness' sake did you write to each other about?"

"You wouldn't find it funny . . . HAVING GOOD TIME AND LYING DOWN? she asked, for example. LYING DOWN WITH PIZZA ON BELLY, I replied. PIZZA BELLY, THATS QUITE COMMON NOW, WOTZ ON PIZZA? she retorted. LITTLE EYES & EARS & NOSES & LIZARD TAILS & OVER IN DISTANCE CAN SEE SOMETHING LIKE TOMATOES, I wrote. ANYTHING MOVING

ON THERE? she wrote. WHOLE THING MOVING CUZ ITS ON MY BELLY, I wrote. DONT EAT IT THEN, she wrote. WONT EAT IT, WILL TRY TO WALK IT OFF, I wrote. WALK WHAT OFF? she asked. THIS CORRESPONDENCE OF OURS, I replied. C.G.J. WOULD SAY THAT ITS A MODERN FORM OF PROJEC-TION, she replied. C.G.J. WAS VAIN EGOCENTRIC, I replied . . ."

"Who's a vain egocentric?" Father interrupted.

"Carl Gustav Jung, she was an intellectual type and was attending some lectures . . . & HE WOULD ALSO SAY THIS EXCHANGE OF MSGS HAS MARKED 6UAL SUBTEXT, she answered. I AGREE, I wrote. JESUS!!! she texted. DONT CALL HIM, FOR THE LAST 2000 YEARS U CAN ONLY LEAVE MSGS ON HIS VOICE MAIL, I wrote back. And she wrote: I WONT, NOT RIGHT, AM SITTING IN BAR AND GAMBLING MACHINE NXT 2 ME KEEPS DISPLAYING SAME UGLY MSG OVER & OVER: 'TRY TO AVOID BALLS CHASING U IN SPIRAL! BALLS OF SAME COLOUR WILL BE ELIMINATED IF U HIT AT LEAST 2 BALLS OF SAME COLOUR. IF U HIT DIFFERENT COLOURED BALLS, YOUR BALL WILL BE INSERTED BETWEEN THEM,' I remember that exactly, because I laughed so hard I knocked my cup of tea over, LAUGHED SO HARD KNOCKED MY TEA OVER, I wrote her . . ."

"Alright, that's enough," Father grumbled, "sorry, but it just doesn't seem that funny to me."

"I know."

"You're not twenty anymore, are you . . . The strange thing is, when you were twenty you behaved like a tired old man and now it's the exact opposite."

"Back then I really had my nose to the grindstone. Nowadays I just cruise along and it's working. That was the greatest discovery of my life . . ."

"What was?"

"That you don't have to try and work out what's going to happen and how in advance."

"Oh, alright then . . . And you didn't even want to see her?"

"Probably did, but this was also interesting."

"I understand, *the mystery*, don't even tell me . . . ," Father waved his arm, "face it, every woman wants two things, to have fun and to take advantage of the situation!"

"Not true about every woman, that's for sure, but we'd spend all night arguing about that."

"Well, maybe not every single woman, you're right there," Father admitted and slowly, very slowly, wiped his whiskers with his pointy grey-blue fingers, first his chin and then his moustache. And for a few seconds I saw what it really means to be a seventy-year-old in this world. But then I forgot it again immediately.

"Maybe you're right after all," I said, "as a matter of fact she did end up blackmailing me."

"Oh okay, and how?" Father perked up.

"At first she was just a little capricious, then she confided some secrets in me, we had a mutual exchange of sincerity, and then out of nowhere there were slight, off-handed reproaches, and suddenly I had a continuous feeling of guilt and didn't even know how it'd happened . . . We even quarrelled a few times and then made up, and there were moments when I felt like we'd just got married."

"So you did see each other!"

"Not till later, this all happened through text messages. It wasn't until about three weeks had passed that I suggested we could meet, and she agreed and wrote: LOOKING FORWARD TO

IT VERY MUCH. And out of sheer joy it was moving on some-where, wherever that might have been, I sent her a joke: AT BREAK OF DAWN LITTLE MARIENKA WALKS INTO KITCHEN AND SEES NAKED MAN STANDING BY FRIDGE. MORNING, R U OUR NEW BABYSITTER? NO, SAYS GUY, IM YOUR NEW MOTHERFUCKER! I sent it and for over an hour the phone was silent. WHAT WAS THAT SUPPOSED 2 MEAN? she messaged back after about an hour. JOKE, I punched. And there was another long silence. So I went to the fridge, found a bottle with some vodka in it, and poured myself a drink. *Motherfucker*, I said to myself, that probably wasn't the most appropriate thing to write. She's got that kid . . ."

"What kid?"

"She has a child . . . After about an hour the phone went beep, beep, beep: AT FIRST I THOUGHT ID FINALLY FOUND SOMEONE WHO UNDERSTANDS ME. BUT IF YOU DONT FIND ME INTERESTING, JUST TELL ME AND WE DONT HAVE TO MEET. K. I was holding the glass and my head was spinning from it all, my heart was pounding and my hands were shaking and I felt like it was the end of a long, artificially pro-longed, emotionally exhausting relationship. WE DONT HAVE 2, I wrote back. I ADMIRE YOUR COMPOSURE, SAILOR BOY, I CANT EVEN PISS U OFF PROPERLY! she answered.

"*Sailor boy?*"

"Yeah, she called me that . . . 'You're wrong there, bitch!' I shouted at the whole flat and smashed the glass against the wall, looked at the shards for a while, and then went to get the dustpan and brush. And while I was getting on with it she wrote: IM NOT INTERESTED IN THE SUPERFICIAL, BUT IN THE SUBCON-SCIOUS, WRITE ME WHAT YOU REALLY FEEL . . . YOU DONT

WANT TO KNOW, I wrote. THATS EXACTLY WHAT I DO WANT TO KNOW! she replied. IN THAT CASE FUCK YOU! I punched and sent. Well, that was basically the end of it . . ."

"Then you weren't being unfaithful, you were just being a dimwit," Father said, "you should have sent her packing immediately."

"I'm no good at that. After all, it's mainly the way you brought me up, this moronic politeness of mine."

"Yeah okay, but with a hysterical woman? It was obvious right away . . . If at least you knew what she looked like, then I could understand."

"I did see what she looked like in the end."

"I thought so!"

"A few months later she wrote to say she'd like to apologise, that she'd been going through a tough time, so finally we did go out to have that coffee. She turned out to be a serious, surprisingly very pretty ginger-haired woman in her early thirties. She told me she was married to a guy who whenever he visits his mother, which he does on a regular basis, can't escape the feeling that *she* is actually his real wife. As a result, she, the thirty-year-old redhead, feels like their daughter. We drank two glasses of wine and went our separate ways."

"It's a bit sad in terms of reality, but it would make a fine short story."

"Except there's no climax whatsoever."

"As with everything that actually happens! You only get a climax in films and stupid books . . . Reality only ends in tears, for goodness' sake!"

"You're just a terrible pessimist, that's all," I said and went to take a leak.

"And what else should I be?" Father objected when I'd come back. "I fooled around a lot too in my day, but there comes a time when you understand that you can't do that forever . . . Did I ever tell you that for forty years now my friends have been calling me Čombe and I don't know why?"

"Čombe? You never told me that."

"Čombe — doesn't matter in the end, really . . . But as far as women are concerned, the one I saw eye to eye with the most was a woman called Lída, I don't think you ever even got to meet her, she used to be, and still is by the way, a highly attractive woman, but a complete loon as well. She used to get these dizzy spells, on account of which she'd spend time at Palata, the home for the partially sighted. But when she happened to be okay she used to be a lot of fun, her best number was the song 'General Laudon Riding through the Village,' she could entertain everyone with that for half an hour or more. She'd also led a hard life. At the start of the eighties she fell in love with some anaesthetist who walked out on her after a year or two and then she emigrated to America where she married a Slovak who was dimwitted but knew how to make money and he got her pregnant. But when she was in the third month of the pregnancy, the anaesthetist got in touch with her, asking her to come back because he couldn't live without her and he was waiting for her. So she packed her things overnight, not caring about anything else, including the fact that she might be sent to prison on arrival, returned to Bohemia and after a couple of weeks the anaesthetist told her he'd made a mistake and was going back to his ex. And Lída didn't know any better than to give herself an abortion using a knitting needle in some tiny one-room flat . . . I only heard about all this from a third party, you understand, I only got to know her personally later on. But I think that must have been the moment when she got everything mixed up in her head."

"With a knitting needle?" I repeated, finally deflating the spheres of noxious iodine-purple and blue light that had gradually engulfed the majority of objects under my steady gaze. Only the Prince Heinrich had resisted. It lay on the table next to Father's right elbow, pointing upwards and refusing to take part in the game. It resembled the blatantly gaping red gob of a fat Italian tenor. A gob ready to swallow Father's head.

"With a knitting needle?" I repeated.

"That's right. But don't tell anyone, you're the only one I've ever told that to."

"And who would I go telling?"

"Well, I don't know, I know you . . . Lída is back in Prague now and I've got a date with her next Monday."

"And what about that plump blonde from Pelhřimov?" I asked.

"Yeah, yeah, I still go to see her every now and then, what's a man got left in life . . . Which for some unknown reason made me think of Kocián, a former colleague of mine from the microbiology department, he was in Munich recently and in a shop window he saw a huge stuffed Dolly Buster, you know who she is, right? So he couldn't resist buying it, brought it to Prague, and when his wife Miluška saw it she flew into a terrible rage and they had an argument and the next day she moved out and a week later she filed for divorce because she said it was the last straw. We all have our trials and tribulations, I guess . . ."

Father made a gesture with his arm and snapped his fingers at the half-naked majorette like an old-fashioned gentleman: "Two more juniper brandies please!"

"Just this once, because it's such a pleasant evening," he said, turning to me, "and stop frowning like a toothless Beelzebub, you in a hurry to get somewhere?"

"I'm not in a hurry to go anywhere," I said. "By the way, the whole time I was a kid I was convinced it was Busy Bob . . ."

And Father burst out laughing, sincerely. For the first time that evening. The last time we'd been out for a beer he didn't laugh once. Or the time before that. Or even the time before that, I'm sure. Not till now. And at something so ridiculous. We drank up, paid the bill, pushed our chairs back, got up, pushed the chairs back in place, made our way through the luminescent smoke to the door, opened it, and walked out into the air.

"You see, it's going to rain, good thing I took my Prince Heinrich," Father praised himself, put his cap on, and bumped into a dustbin. "I reckon Kohout would burst with anger if he knew that some old man was wearing *his* cap . . ."

"What?"

"Well, it was his cap to start off with, at least that's what you told me."

"Oh, did I give it you?"

"Of course you did, when you were living in Smíchov, and you claimed it had been Kohout's."

"I guess that's the case, then."

"I guess so, because when I met her she kept looking up at the cap, in a strange sort of way . . ."

"When you met who?"

"That Rezeda, your ex, it was a few years back and all . . . I met her by chance on the street and she came up to me, staring at the cap, and right out she said that she never liked me because I behave like an *idiot* and I'm an alcoholic and a disgrace or something, I don't remember exactly . . . And that you take after me."

"You should've slapped the rude bitch, she's ridiculous!" I shouted into the darkness, waving away a cloud of tiresome flies.

"For goodness' sake, the type of woman who thinks the world's a stage isn't worth getting all worked up about, maybe I am an alcoholic, but that doesn't mean I'm going to confess it to some pretentious brat," Father said. "Oh yeah, but back to my nickname, as I was saying before, thing is I recently decided to find out how it came about, so I asked my friends and they said: 'Oh, Čombe, it was Gustík Mimra who came up with it way back when, but he's dead now, but wait, young Pozděna might know, oh, but he's dead too, oh well, I'm afraid I don't know, Ivan, I've been calling you that for thirty-five years and I've no idea what it means . . .' And the lesson is that if there's something you want to know, you should ask straightaway . . . Oh well, what are we going to do? You feel like walking for a bit longer?"

I was looking at two shadows hopping on the pavement in the yellow light of the streetlamps. One of them is tall, the other has short legs, the ubiquitous satchel in his hand. Two bipeds, living their two not particularly remarkable lives in the middle of the capital of one not particularly large republic at the very end of the highly successful era of the species *Homo sapiens*.

"What are you thinking about?" Father asked.

"Me? Nothing, why?"

"You're silent."

"And what are you thinking about?"

"Nothing either, really, nothing and everything, about what a mess this world is, about people, Ivana, Misha, Misha calls me *Grandfather Ivan*, recently I took her to the museum to see the rorqual, hadn't been there for years . . ."

"The rorqual?"

"Yep, the skeleton in the National Museum, you know, the fin whale, the second largest whale on earth . . . I used to take you there when you were little, then I used to take Ivana and now Misha, you could never get enough of looking at the moa and you were disgusted by the arachnid Galeodes araneoides, Ivana liked the lemurs and tarsiers best and she detested the squid preserved in formaldehyde, whereas Misha likes everything, she's still little . . . But imagine this! There we were standing beneath the rorqual in the middle of a heat wave, and as I was looking up I noticed the bones were still sweating, still exuding fat!"

"Really? They must have been hanging there for at least a hundred years."

"Longer in fact, the Norwegians sold it to us for two thousand five hundred gold coins in 1880, the money came from a collection organised by Frič, the zoologist, not the movie director . . . And having transported the whale here, for a long time they couldn't find a pot big enough to boil the bones in, until in the end they steam-boiled them in the Ringhoffer factory, the residents of Smíchov protested back then because of the ungodly stench . . . And there you have it! They didn't do it right, there's still fat in those bones!"

We walked past blocks of flats. *"Cruel is the northern wind, you should know that, my love, I'll place golden bars at your feet, though I might not be back . . ."* boomed from a number of open windows lit by blue pulsating light.

"For all its real stupidity, this film has a certain charm — melancholic, almost metaphysical," I said. "I have to watch it every time it's on, even if I don't really feel like it, but somehow I have to . . ."

"What film?"

"Run Waiter Run."

"Oh, right, but I wonder if you know that the greatest actor of all time was Charles Laughton?" Father asked. "And do you know why? Because he studied each role by learning the *walk* first, he learned to walk like the character and then he did the rest . . ."

"I've only ever seen him in *The Hunchback of Notre Dame*. By the way, you know Granddad gave you an earful because you let me watch it on TV and I almost vomited I was so frightened: *I am not a human being, I am not an animal either, what am I in fact* . . . I couldn't sleep for a week after that!"

"Really?" Father said, a hint of joy in his voice.

"Yeah, it was the first time I heard Granddad really shouting . . . It was an Athos TV, the kind that when you turned it off a little spot in the middle of the screen would shine for twenty minutes, it looked exactly like a star above a forest . . . *The Hunchback of Notre Dame*, I was four or five years old at the time, but I've never seen any other film with Laughton in it."

"Neither have I . . . Hell, I could really do with a bite to eat! I wonder if that thought ever occurs to those, you know . . . what did you say they were called? The ones who live near the Ganges?"

"The Shaivas. I used to know a guy called Kukačka, a real cuckoo, from Letňany, who wanted to taste human meat for so long that he actually ended up doing so."

"You don't say. Is he a doctor?"

"No he's not, but a friend of his was. And one time they were stupidly egging each other on to cook human flesh. So the doctor brought a piece of a girl who had been run over by a car and they chopped it up back at Kukačka's place. Then they stood there looking at it, apparently it was beautifully red, clean, lovely meat, but they suddenly lost the nerve to just roast it as it was. Kukačka remembered a recipe his mother used for beef stew. They chopped up onion, garlic, carrot, made a vinegar marinade, added some bay leaves, thyme, allspice, salt and pepper, chopped the meat up into cubes and left it to marinade for two days . . ."

"How do you know all this so exactly? You weren't there as well, for Christ's sake, were you?"

"No I wasn't . . . They left it to marinade and then drank for two days so they'd have the courage to go through with it, because they were less and less keen with every passing minute. So in the end they got the meat out, fried it in oil, and then they gradually added the rest of the marinade, stewing it until they had a sort of ragout, a sort of human goulash. They put it on the table and sat down, passed the plates out, hesitating for a moment, but apparently it gave off a wonderful smell, so they knocked back one more shot and ate it."

"Did they like it?"

"They loved it, it seems. But then they sobered up and it started to get to them. From that day on they couldn't stand each other. Every time they met their aversion to one another grew. So they swore never to tell anyone and didn't see each other for a year. But during that year Kukačka lost his marbles, left his job at the research institute, broke up with his girlfriend, became a recluse, and in the end got a job as a tram driver. I ran into him a few years after this took place. I was on the No. 22 and suddenly I see that it's being driven by a noticeably skinnier Kukačka, so I did the route with him four times and we talked. And up at Pohořelec, at the last stop, he let the cat out of the bag. He said he couldn't get it out of his mind. That he never goes out anywhere. That he only eats porridge. That he can't walk past a butcher's without feeling sick. That I'm the first person in all those years he's confided in."

"I understand where he's coming from," Father said, "I used to get pangs of conscience just from eating the lab rabbits at the institute, it's just prejudice what we consider okay to eat and what we don't . . . But how come you remember that recipe so precisely?"

"Because up there in Pohořelec Kukačka got in a weird rut and kept describing it to me over and over. First they removed *the onion* from the marinade, put it in *the oil* in the pan and when it had *sweated down*, they added *the meat*. They put the marinade in a pan *next to it* to cook and only once it had *reduced down* to about half the volume they started to *add the marinade* to the meat. At the end they were supposed to add *cream* but it seemed silly to have a girl with cream sauce, so they didn't put it in . . . I was pretty frightened of him at the time because it was clear that he really did have a few screws loose. So that's one reason . . ."

"Alright, and the other?"

"Well, the recipe got so stuck in my mind I couldn't help trying it with braising steak, and it really is delicious."

"That's another lovely story, that is," Father shook his head, "and what's up with this Cockatoo of yours now?"

"Kukačka? I've no idea, I guess he's living somewhere. He was always more of a quiet type and the episode with the girl in the goulash was the most significant event of his life."

At the end of the street we stopped by a bush, taking up positions on opposite sides, Father on one side, me on the other.

"So, when do we go out for a beer again?" I called over to him.

"You're the one that's never got time, call me, I've always got time for my kids . . . People have been calling me Čombe for years now, it's a nickname, and I have no idea why . . . I know, I've said that already . . . But tell me this, do you recognise this bush?"

"What?"

"Do you know what the bush we're pissing on is called . . . !?"

I could make out some leaves shaking in front me. Branches of some kind. Berries on them. An unkempt patch of grass bordered by piles of gravel. Dark buildings resembling cliffs, towering over us on all sides.

"*Pamba Palace slumbers*
Alvezura dozes
Alhambra falls asleep
Estremadura is sleeping . . ." I recited to the buildings.

"What is that you're saying?"

"Pamba Palace slumbers, Alvezura dozes, Alhambra falls asleep, Estremadura is sleeping!"

"I know, but where does it come from?"

"If only I knew . . ."

"Alright then," Father said, swaying, "and do you at least know what the bush is?"

"I don't."

"You should know this by now, *alder buckthorn*, otherwise known as *black dogwood* . . ."

"Aha."

"It's part of the buckthorn family . . ."

"Hmm."

"The bark is used as a laxative . . ."

"Right."

"Yep, laxatives are important, these days senna pods constitute the most important thing in the world for me! I couldn't exist at all without them . . ."

"Really?"

"Absolutely . . . You've no idea how joyful it is void oneself properly!"

"That's exactly what Grandmother used to say when I was squatting on the potty beneath those flamingos of yours: 'Honzík, whatever you do, don't rush! Void yourself properly!' Well, after all these years I've managed to do that pretty well in the end. I've been fairly empty of late."

"Aha, you're talking about the soul again . . ."

"There's always need to talk about the soul! Look around you in the street, or in the metro, just take a moment to look around and you'll get the creeps!"

"From what?"

"The freak show."

"I can see it alright, but it doesn't surprise me one bit, from the moment something takes a wrong turn on the evolutionary path it just keeps going down it and there's no way of turning it back . . . Just look at all the growth anomalies around, all those deformations and obvious mutations and aberrations, look at the current U.S. president, with a mug like that the most you could accomplish a hundred years ago was doing the milk rounds in a loony bin! By that I mean to say that if we consider the body to be normal today, what state must the *soul* be in! But knowing you, you probably wanted to say something about yourself . . ."

"Not really."

"About what then?"

"About how difficult it is to stay focused. To think."

"Yep, that changes like the weather. Neurons aren't made to last, even after two or three beers you can feel how hapless they are . . . In fact, the whole body is badly designed and badly constructed, but the nervous system is the worst part of it . . . But why do you need to think? How about just reflecting, isn't that enough?"

"I never stop reflecting but nothing good comes of it. I reflect and I ponder and in my very bones I can feel how I'm slowly and gently turning into a boring, stupid dickhead."

"I've known much worse cases, for example there's a guy called Mirek Panoška, who even though a doctor of science either starts or finishes everything he says with: 'Cunt like moss, dick like steel, once and forever united together' and just imagine hearing that fifty times in one night! But this learned philosopher is nothing compared to a certain Reguš from Rychvald, who after two rums would say nothing all evening but 'New Years Eve by the TV in the arms of the woman you love. Priceless!' "

Rolling his eyes and strangely puffing up his cheeks, Father said: "I wouldn't say you're boring, maybe unnecessarily serious."

"Serious. Me?"

"Well, you haven't told a joke as far as I remember . . . Good thing you don't talk about God like Grandmother, she used to believe in some kind of God, but in her interpretation it was a sort of improved Jára Pospíšil or Charles Boyer, the kind of person whose shoes are always clean."

Father said, puffing up his cheeks under his white beard. In the eerie lamplight he looked like a purple and wild Masaryk.

"I don't like jokes," I said.

"And what do you like?"

"What do I like? I just like stories about things that have actually happened in this world."

"Tell me one then."

"That's all I've been doing . . . Not too long ago I was staying with some friends of mine at their cottage in this beautiful wild valley over behind Golčův Jeníkov and everything inside this cottage was really massive, a raised bed made of planks that a mammoth could sleep in, a table that could take the weight of a roasted rhinoceros, and above the table there was a chandelier on chains made from a tree stump, a piece of wood the shape of an octopus that must have weighed a hundred kilos and extended over half the room. And they explained to me that we were in a cottage built by their uncle and this uncle was a very kind man but he also weighed a hundred and ninety kilos . . .”

"That's like the two of us put together and a crate of beers on top!”

"This uncle had a habit of going on walks in the surrounding countryside because he didn't go to work, he was on a disability pension, because who would employ a great hulk of a man like that. As he got older he kept stuffing himself and got fatter and fatter until it took him half a day just to get out of bed. By that time he only went out to the meadow above the cottage. He'd just go round it twice and then go back home. And one time, apparently, he was so tired that he dropped down in the middle of the meadow for a breather, but when he wanted to move on he realised he just couldn't get up on his own . . .”

"That's sad more than anything.”

"Hold on a sec . . . For a while he tried to get up, rolling around from one side to the other, groaning, but then he fell asleep from the exertion. But some tourists saw him and went to take a look at the giant, out of curiosity. The uncle was snoring so hard it was making the mullein plants bend over, but they thought the man was choking and having some terrible fit, and they tried to revive him, but the uncle just kept snoring, his throat rattling and he was drooling and exhaling loudly . . .”

"Oh well, people just won't leave a good man alone in peace!"

"So these hysterical tourists called an ambulance. It arrived, the medics ran out, pounced on the uncle and started tending to him . . ."

"People, oh well!"

"And that woke him up in the end . . ."

"No wonder!"

"When the uncle opened his eyes and saw the crowd around him he asked them to help him get up, thanked them all, and went home," I said. "See, you're laughing!"

"Oh, come on, why should I laugh, he was a poor bastard! And what happened to him in the end?"

"In the end he died."

"Well, there you go, and I'm supposed to laugh at that?"

"So what are you doing then?"

"Grinning."

"And why?"

"No reason, just like that. My facial muscles are the last of my muscles that still function fairly well. But let me tell you one thing . . . All my life I've tried to be discreet and recently I've had the feeling that in my old age I might just end up in psychiatric care like other people . . ."

"How's that?"

"I've been getting the urge to say things in public that can't really be justified . . ."

"Like what for instance?"

"Well, the other day some woman bumped into me in the doorway when I was coming out of the supermarket at Špořilov and she started swearing at me, saying that I'd bumped into her . . . So I grabbed her by the ears, I don't know what got into me, and said: 'You might just be interested in the news that people the world over give priority to those who are leaving a place, you inbred hagbag!' And she started screaming that she was going to sue me and grabbed some old bat to act as a witness, asking if she'd heard me call her a hagbag! Strange thing is, the shrew didn't particularly seem to mind that I'd grabbed her by the ears."

"That's no reason to go to the loony bin. You should get a state decoration for fostering the development of interpersonal relations!"

"Thing is though, I've said much worse to complete strangers . . ."

"Like what?"

"I'll tell you another time, I'd need to have another juniper brandy for that . . . Listen, but where did you get hold of a Chinese woman . . . ? You said you'd been with some Chinese woman, didn't you . . . ?"

"I did . . . But listen to this, my friends' kids put their pet tomcat in the washing machine, closed the door, and set the programme to hot wash."

"And how old are they?"

"Six and eight."

"That's humankind for you, I hope they at least got a good hiding . . . But why are you telling me this?"

"Because it's a report on the state of the world and because I don't want to talk about women anymore."

"And why not, for goodness' sake?"

"Because it's the same thing over and over," I said.

Before my eyes I saw an image of myself sitting on the river-bank in front of the Rudolfinum, holding an open book, but

I'm not reading. I'm staring at the world around me because it's May and suddenly from behind the building a strange pack appears: at the head run three disgusting pink poodles with bright bows around their necks, looking like prematurely degenerate schoolgirls, behind them trots a deranged salivating collie wearing a silk golden-green aristocratic waistcoat, and behind all that comes Father, holding the leashes with the expression of someone about to doze off. Before my eyes I have a vivid image of my body shifting on the bench so that I stay out of sight, cowering behind a tree trunk. The image is in sharp focus and precise in every detail. Only after many years did he admit that the menagerie belonged to some ex-model.

"That's humankind for you," Father repeated. "No one gives a toss about the fact that the cetaceans are almost extinct, but everyone's interested in the fact that a ninety-year-old woman got raped, that was in the papers this morning . . . Are you even aware, for goodness' sake, how many *sperm whales* are left on the entire planet?"

"People have been manufacturing their own version of nature for ages now, it suits them better than the original. The world has simply disappeared. How many sperm whales are left?"

"That sounded like you were quoting someone."

"I was quoting some guy called Serres and I don't have a clue who he is. How many sperm whales are left?"

"I know you like the sort of talk that pretends life means something . . ."

"Doesn't it?"

"Of course not, at least not in any higher sense!"

"Well, alright. How many sperm whales are left?"

"Not many, that's all . . . Just tell me this, though . . ."

"What?"

"What happened with that Chinese girl . . ."

"She stayed at my place for a few days."

We found ourselves in another street and then another, where another line of buildings was waving its open windows to the darkness. *"And for our final item this evening . . . can film made in . . . taking place in . . . and only Matthew Bennell and his partner Elizabeth realise the terrible danger, but by this time the aliens are everywhere . . ."* a carefree female voice announced to the reddened sky.

"And she was someone you knew, or what?" Father asked. "That doesn't make any sense to me, how could a Chinese woman be living at your place . . ."

"It happens."

"The one thing I regret about you is that you're always fabricating, in fact I've always regretted that . . . Why do you always have to make things up . . ."

"I haven't been making things up for years now, damn it! It's your problem if you still see me as a little runt! Just don't ask me about anything then, I don't have to tell stories to anyone, I don't particularly care for it!"

"Anyone . . . Well alright, then . . ."

"You're my father, I know. So either believe me, or don't ask!"

"You could at least explain to me where you got hold of that Chinese girl, after all there's an explanation for everything in this world . . . I wonder if you know that your grandfather originally came from a village called Vlčeves, you remember that in case I die, I've been on overtime for a long time as it is . . . A decent person should get cancer at the age of sixty at the very latest and get out of here . . . Vlčeves, it's the other side of Tábor . . . That's also why he could ride a horse . . . Hey listen, and where are we in fact?"

I looked around for signs. "Chittussi Street," I said.

"I know who Chittussi was . . ."

"Well then, it's a street named after Chittussi."

"That's all very well, Chittussi Street . . . But *where?*"

"What do you mean, where? Chittussi Street, that's all, not far from the main street."

"I get that, damn it, Chittussi Street . . . But what *town* are we in?"

"In Prague, where would we be," I said.

A second, maybe two, went by. Only then did it sink in and I got a jolt.

"Oh well, you see . . ." Father said in the direction of the blind wall of a building, "I never did sleep with a Japanese woman, that simply didn't work out for me . . . That's how it is, oh well . . . Prague, I know . . . I'm an old man now, I forget every time, my mind goes blank, that's all . . ."

"Doesn't matter, let's go catch the metro."

"Alright, I guess it's time to go . . . Listen, you're not angry are you?"

"No."

"And are you at least a little bit happy? I'd really like you to be at least a little bit happy . . ."

"Sure I am, of course, yes."

"Yes *what?*"

"Yes I'm happy, damn it!"

"You're irate, that's for sure, do you know who you take after?"

"I do."

"Well, there you go then . . . And let me tell you another thing, at least in the old days the shops had intelligible names, but now? What the hell's *DIY Paradise? Partypoopers?* I'd be too embarrassed to even walk into a place called that . . . There's a shop called *Tip Top*, I don't even want to know what I could buy there . . . Probably best if we look for a taxi now . . ."

"Okay."

"Is there anything you need . . . Anything you'd like?"

"No, I've got everything."

Yugoslav Partisans Street was glistening like an eggshell. I waved down a taxi, and Father got in.

"Spořilov," I said into the driver's window.

"That's right, Spořilov, if you'd be so kind," Father said, awkwardly trying to close the door behind him.

The driver leaned over, grabbed the door handle, closed the door again, and started the ignition. Father managed his usual parting gesture, raising his arm and waving it as if he were saying *forever onward* while looking somewhere beneath the dashboard. At one time this used to confuse me, later it infuriated me (what kind of dad have you got who can't look anyone in the eye!), but only now was I astonished to realise that it was an expression of an almost frightening timidity, one that never found a suitable way to take part in the chortling game of whist, the pot-bellied card match game, any of those jovial games, the whooping and howling and snapping of fingers and dishonest yodelling that's forever echoing all around us.

Watching the lights of the receding taxi, I could see a piece of white raincoat caught in the door, flapping behind it. I could see Father's head, staring ahead. A head topped with the greasy Prince Heinrich.

You'll be nicer to him next time . . . the demon started babbling again: You'll be more patient . . . ! He's your father . . . ! The man who raised you . . . ! He's the only person in the world who has patience with you . . . !

I set off through the side streets roughly in the direction of the traffic circle at Victory Square. I suddenly felt the need to get a coffee somewhere.

He's your *old man* . . . ! The demon added wood to the fire, let's get that fire blazing: Who knows how many times you'll get to see him again . . . ! You prick . . . ! You pathetic . . . ! You ingrate . . . !

I watched the uneven surface of the road rush beneath my feet.

At the same time I began to recall an event that took place a lot more than thirty years ago. Back then he brought me a box full of matchbox cars from somewhere. I was mad with joy and gave him a kiss, and he objected in a confused sort of way: "Alright, come on, you're overdoing it a little, aren't you, men don't kiss each other, you're a big lad now . . ." He probably meant it simply in a rhetorical sort of way as part of my upbringing. But that was the last kiss he ever got from me in his life. He would've wanted one after all those years when he was lying in the hospital waiting for his operation and I was standing over him with a bag of oranges. But by then it couldn't be done.

As I was walking through the little park away from U Pětníka restaurant, I noticed something strange. A pale, scrawny bloke was sitting in a treetop next to the playground, absorbed in thought, letting fall gobs of spit. Whether I wanted to or not, I had to walk by him. As I was passing, he jerked his head, throwing his hair to the side, and gazed at me with bleary eyes: "Don't ask me why I'm up here . . . ptooey . . . All you lot ever do is bullshit on . . . ptooey . . . Bullshit and more bullshit, that's all you know . . . Just go your way and let me be . . . ptooey . . . Fuck off . . . ," he was saying to me, and a long trail of spit hit the dry lawn.

"I wonder if you at least know the name of the tree you're sitting in?" I wanted to say, but stayed silent instead. For one thing, I didn't know myself: I can recognise an oak, a lime, a birch, an aspen, a maple, poplar, yew, willow, most of the main fruit trees, of course I recognise a spruce, larch, fir and pine, sometimes a common maple and, if one were around, even a gingko. But that's it.

When I reached the corner I looked around. The bloke was squatting on the branch, spitting through his legs at regular intervals. Above him revolved the black bowl of the sky. In the distance beyond the horizon a silent lightning flash appeared.

I walked along the traffic circle, up Buzulucká Street, opened the doors of Bistro Olin on the corner, and sat on the bench by the window. Two elderly couples were sitting directly opposite each other and having a hushed conversation. The waiter, who I knew by sight, was leaning on the bar and watching TV.

A really young girl was sitting at the table in the corner, looking bored. She was puffing on her cigarette and sipping wine. She had a carefully trimmed fringe and beneath that a pair of green, attentive, intelligent — in a nutshell, ruthless — eyes. Suddenly she let her head fall to one side, looked at me and twisted one side of her lips a little. I realised I'd been gawping at her for a good five minutes. I shrugged my shoulders. The girl shrugged her shoulders. I twisted my finger in my ear hole. The girl located her ear in her hair and did the same. I yawned. The girl also yawned. I stretched my neck, turned my head stiffly, and looked at her with a slow glassy-eyed glare I had learned many years before from Max Schreck in his most celebrated role.

"That's meeeental . . ." the girl shrieked, she couldn't have been over twenty, "what was that?"

"What do you reckon?" I wasn't going to be formal with her.

"Some kind of Dracula."

"Vampire," I specified.

"And why . . . ?"

"Why what?"

"Why is part of your tooth missing, mister?"

Mister. Aha.

"Because I didn't move fast enough."

The girl laughed: "You have to sharpen your reactions!"

"That's true, that I must . . ." I said and gazed into the scintillating darkness beyond the window. All of a sudden I remembered that I was forty-two years old, and that I had Hanka at home, the best woman I'd ever met whom I definitely did not deserve.

"Hi there, what'll it be?" said the waiter I knew by sight, leaning over me. There was nothing particularly striking or interesting about him, besides the fact that it was generally known he wore women's underwear instead of boxers. Other than that he was apparently entirely okay. When asked why he wears panties he always answered that they're simply more comfortable.

"Double espresso and I'll pay straightaway," I answered.

ABOUT THE AUTHOR

Emil Hakl was born in Prague in 1958. A graduate of
the Jaroslav Ježek Conservatorium, he worked at a
number of manual-labor jobs under Communism,
during which time he wrote poetry and dramatiza-
tions of literature for amateur theater. Having been
a copywriter for an advertising agency in the 1990s,
by the end of the decade he decided to devote himself to writing and has published a volume of poetry,
three novels, and two collections of short stories
since.

ABOUT THE TRANSLATOR

Marek Tomin was born in Prague and grew up in
England, where his family found refuge after being
exiled in 1980 by the Communist regime. A graduate
of Oxford University, he lives in Prague where he
works as a freelance translator, journalist, documen-
tary producer, and contemporary art curator. His
translations include *Time is a Mid-Night Scream* by
Pavel Zajíček.

OF KIDS & PARENTS

by Emil Hakl

Translated by Marek Tomin from the Czech original
O rodičích a dětech (Prague: Argo, 2002)

Design by Jed Slast
Set in Futura Condensed / Janson
Cover and frontispiece photos by Marek Tomin

FIRST EDITION

Published in 2008 by
TWISTED SPOON PRESS
P.O. Box 21 – Preslova 12
150 21 Prague 5, Czech Republic
info@twistedspoon.com / www.twistedspoon.com

Printed and bound in the Czech Republic by PB Tisk

Distributed to the trade by

SCB DISTRIBUTORS
15608 South New Century Drive
Gardena, CA 90248-2129
USA
toll free: 1-800-729-6423
www.scbdistributors.com

CENTRAL BOOKS
99 Wallis Road
London, E9 5LN
United Kingdom
tel: 0845 458 9911
www.centralbooks.com